REVENGE OF THE WILDCAT

REVENGE
OF THE WILDCAT

Griselda Gifford

Illustrated by Mary Rayner

CANONGATE · KELPIES

First published in 1989 by
Canongate Publishing Limited.
First published by Canongate Kelpies in 1991.

© Griselda Gifford 1989
© Illustrations Mary Rayner 1989

British Library Cataloguing in Publication Data

Gifford, Griselda, *1931–*
Revenge of the Wildcat
I. Title   II. Rayner, Mary
823′.914 [J]

ISBN 0-86241-334-6

The publishers acknowledge subsidy of the Scottish Arts Council
towards the publication of this volume.

Printed and bound in Great Britain by
Cox and Wyman, Reading.

CANONGATE PRESS PLC
14 FREDERICK STREET, EDINBURGH EH2 2HB

To Mark, Nicola and the real Lucy.

CHAPTER ONE

'There's the Loch,' said Mr. Carter.

He stopped the car on the crest of the hill and pointed down at a great stretch of water like the sea.

Tim Carter wiped a patch in the steamed-up window and saw a dark arm of land running out into the Loch, ending in a crouching black lump. Mountains, some snowcapped, surrounded three sides of the Loch and in the distance, the greyness of the water melted into the darker grey of the rainfilled sky.

He clutched at the little dog, Lucy, and she licked his face. The Loch was a sinister dream-place, brooding angrily as if it did not want the Carter family on their first holiday in Scotland.

'It looks unfriendly,' Tim said.

'Wet,' said his sister Becca. 'And I'm hungry.' He thought that she galloped through food as she galloped through life.

'Lovely mountains for climbing,' said Dad, always

optimistic. 'Which way now?'

'First left and then down a long drive,' Mum said, looking at Mrs. Macpherson's letter, which she had taken from her file marked HOLIDAY. Tim thought that her life was all lists and plans. He wondered if she had any time left for dreaming.

They drove down the road and then between ancient stone gateposts with what looked like stone cats on either side.

As they bumped along the uneven road, Mum called, 'Look out!'

Dad stopped to let a very wet, shaggy cow lurch out of the way.

'Cows, you see,' he said. 'We'll be able to help with the milking.'

'It's all done by machines now,' Becca said in her most squashing voice. Tim felt sorry for Dad.

Mr. Carter was not to be squashed. 'Probably not right up here,' he said. 'And we can help make the hay . . .' As any hay there might be must be sodden and flat in this rain, Tim didn't think it likely.

A long grey house lay ahead at the edge of the Loch. Part of the roof had fallen in. 'Perhaps it's the wrong address,' Becca said.

'I can see smoke coming out of a chimney,' said Tim. 'It might be a haunted house,' he said hopefully. If they had to come to Scotland where there was no beach for him to make sand motorways, there ought to be a good ghost.

'Ghosts don't exist,' said Mum.

Dad stopped the car on the weedy forecourt and they got out. Lucy ran off at once, straight through the open front door.

She rushed out again, chased by the largest dog Tim had ever seen.

'He'll eat her!' he said as Lucy stopped running and lay on her back, her short legs in the air. The dog sniffed her.

10

Tim approached it with his hand outstretched. No animal had ever scared him.

'Don't touch it!' said Mum but the dog sniffed Tim's hand and wagged its long tail slowly. It looked at Tim with dark, intelligent eyes. It had a steel grey coat, a long bearded muzzle and silky dark ears.

'I think it's an Irish Wolfhound,' he said, remembering his dog book.

Mum knocked at the front door, which seemed silly as she was half-standing in the hall already. Tim noticed the brass knocker had a cat's head on it.

The rain, which had almost stopped, now began to fall even harder. 'I'm getting wet!' Becca complained.

'I think we ought to go in,' said Mum.

'Mrs. Macpherson's probably just slipped out to feed the animals,' Dad said.

Inside, the hall was large and dim and it smelled of woodsmoke and damp. Mum called out again, 'Mrs. Macpherson!' Her voice echoed into the silence. She tried the oak door to her right but it was locked.

'Probably leads to the hole-in-the-roof bit,' Dad said.

'Or they've locked in a mad aunt whom they feed at night,' Tim suggested. Or perhaps there was an invalid child, pale and sickly, whom he could rescue. He saw himself helping the child grow strong. It was a story he'd read somewhere . . .

The others had gone into the kitchen on the left and he followed. There was an old-fashioned black range, a big scrubbed table and two deep, narrow windows, overlooking the Loch.

Mum took the lid off the pan on the range. 'Stew,' she said. 'Where can she be?'

'Perhaps she's been captured by burglars and is lying bound and gagged in a cupboard,' Tim suggested hopefully. After all, surely one day a proper adventure might come his way? Then he could be resourceful and brave and show he wasn't just Becca's rather weedy younger brother.

'You did confirm the date, darling?' Mum asked. She gave Dad one of her looks. Tim thought it was unlike her to leave the booking to Dad, who was so vague. Mum thrived on dates and diaries.

'I did, and I remember posting the letter on the way to work. I don't always forget things,' he added.

'I'm starving.' Becca dived into a breadbin, bringing out a huge loaf. 'Funny shape,' she said, hacking at it with a knife.

'Becca . . .' Mum called but it was too late. Dad said when Becca was hungry she behaved like a human vacuum cleaner.

'Awful wholemeal stuff,' she said with her mouth full. 'I suppose they can't get sliced bread up here.'

'Wholemeal's better for you,' Mum said, bustling them out of their wet clothes and then spreading anoraks around the range. Lucy and the wolfhound curled up together in front of the warmth. Lucy looked like a little hairy puppy beside the big dog.

Becca, prevented by Mum from finishing the loaf, complained every five minutes that she was hungry. Dad murmured on about the lovely atmosphere and Mum looked restless.

Tim stared out of the window. The rain was lifting a little now and he stared out across the heather. From here, he could see that the house wasn't right at the edge of the Loch after all: steep heathery ground fell away to a kind of shore. He saw now, too, that there were ruins at the end of the arm of land, high up on a rocky hill. The Loch was ruffled by wind, grey and huge.

'Maybe there's a monster like the Loch Ness one,' he said. He could *almost* see a long dark shape, writhing and rearing . . . 'Writhing and rearing . . .' he murmured, liking the words.

'It's a sea Loch,' Dad said. 'On the north side, there's a gap where the sea comes in.' He looked over Tim's shoulder. 'You could find a small shark, perhaps.'

Tim preferred to think of a proper monster, humping its serpentine way along. He was planning a monster hunt one moonlit night when a soft voice behind him said, 'Oh, I'm so sorry, but my son has disappeared.'

He turned round to see a tall, ginger-haired woman. She wore an anorak and jeans clung wetly to her thin legs.

'Oh dear,' Mum said. 'Can we help?'

Mrs. Macpherson fended off the wolfhound's welcoming bounce. 'Down, Tara!' she said. Then she hurried to stir the stew. 'I suppose I'm being silly,' she said. 'After all, Alan is eleven but he's been gone all day and not done his work round the place either. Well, to be fair, he had milked our cow but he was gone by the time I got up.'

'Did he take food?' Mum asked.

'Probably he's just wandered off and forgot the time,' Dad said. It was the kind of thing Dad would do, especially in the country when he was bird-watching.

'He just took some bread,' said Mrs. Macpherson. Becca stared at the bread-bin and went pink. 'And it's not like him, to forget the time. He's quite good about helping me in this big place.'

'Have you tried his friends?' Dad suggested.

She shook her head. 'His best friend is away down south and Alan's been a bit of a loner since . . . well, lately. Of course I didn't worry too much until he missed his lunch. He's always so hungry.'

At the word 'hungry' Becca made a face and Mum frowned at her but not before Mrs. Macpherson had seen it. 'I expect you're all longing for a meal after a journey like that,' she said. 'You must think I am the most terrible landlady. I expect Alan will turn up soon and then he'll get a piece of my mind.'

She moved about jerkily, laying the table and removing

some overdone-looking baked potatoes from the oven. 'And of course do please go up to your rooms first,' she added, darting ahead on her thin, bird-like legs.

The staircase and banisters were made of carved dark wood and Tim stroked the cat's head carved at the end. Mrs. Macpherson stopped on the upstairs landing and explained the end door led to the ruined part of the house. It was sealed off, or held up, by battens of wood nailed across it. There was a bucket on the landing, catching drips of water and the damp had made the wallpaper in his room a most interesting pattern, rather like a map of Africa. He heard Mrs. Macpherson making apologetic noises as she showed the others their rooms but he was pleased with his, for his window looked out of the back of the house, at the Loch. A watery gleam of sunshine shot out from the dark clouds and lit the island, as if on purpose, and now he saw that there was water over the arm bit. That's where he would hide—on the island.

Mum called him and he went downstairs reluctantly. 'Have you looked on that island place?' he asked Mrs. Macpherson as she ladled out the stew.

'Alan's strictly forbidden to go there,' she said. 'The ruins are dangerous.'

'What ruins are they?' Becca asked, staring hungrily at the stew.

'They belong to us,' she answered. 'It was a small castle once, then the English set fire to it after the battle of Culloden. They fired this house too, but it was rebuilt. Then there was a bad storm last year and part of the roof fell in. We just can't afford repairs at the moment. That's why the door to that part is locked.'

Of course she *would* say that if there was a mad aunt or a sick child locked up there. 'Is there a ghost?' Tim asked.

She gave him a strange look. 'Events from the past cast their shadows on the present,' she said mysteriously. 'I haven't seen one myself.'

14

Then she became ordinary and handed round the stew. Becca ate as if she had never seen food before but Tim was thinking of ghosts and hid his cooling meat under the baked potato-skin. Mrs. Macpherson didn't sit down at all and Tim felt her tenseness as she moved round the room, from table to stove.

Becca had two helpings of apple pie with cream 'from our cow' said Mrs. Macpherson.

Dad's spectacles glinted enthusiastically and Tim guessed he had to stop himself asking about milking.

When they had finished, Mum said they would all help look for Alan. 'I can't possibly let you . . .' said Mrs. Macpherson but Mum started to organise. Nobody had a chance when Mum was organising.

'Maybe he's gone further than you think,' she said. 'We could drive slowly along and keep a look-out or ask people.'

'I haven't been far,' said Mrs. Macpherson. 'My car's just given out today. I shall have to take it to the garage but they do charge so much.'

'I can help there,' Dad said proudly. The one practical thing he could do was to mend cars.

'Well, where shall we look first?' Mum asked. 'And what does he look like?'

'He's tall and thin, red-haired like me. And he walks with a limp,' Mrs. Macpherson added slowly. 'It might be worth asking in the village or he could be in the valley below the house, where the burn flows into the Loch. It's easy to hide there, among the big rocks and bushes. He might have had a fall . . . his leg . . .' She paused. 'Of course I've called and called . . .'

It was settled. Mr. Carter would drive to the village and make enquiries while picking up Mrs. Macpherson's shopping. Mum would go with Mrs. Macpherson to the ravine and search properly, with Tara to help. She asked Tim and Becca to come with her but Becca wanted to go with her father. 'I'll look on my own,' Tim said. He had an idea at the back of his mind.

'Oh no, you might get lost,' Mum said.

'He's so dreamy—remember that time at the Zoo?' Becca laughed.

Tim glared at her. 'That wasn't my fault. It was yours, staying at the lion house so long.'

Mum stopped them quarrelling and Becca got into the car with Dad. 'I think you'd better come with us, Tim,' Dad said.

'I've a bit of a tummy-ache,' he lied.

'Don't be such a wimp. You've always got tummy-ache,' said Becca. He wanted to hit her big, rosy face. Becca was never ill.

'Let him stay and rest,' said Dad. 'It's been a long drive.' He started the car.

'Not another stomach-ache!' Mum said. 'And you hardly ate anything.' She and Mrs. Macpherson were putting on anoraks and boots.

'I'll be OK,' Tim said. He grabbed Lucy, who wanted to follow Tara.

He waited until the two women walked away, their heads just showing above the heather as they went down the steep slope to the valley with Tara loping along beside them.

The house suddenly felt very empty and old. He shivered as he thought of the mad aunt or the pale child shut up so near and hurried out of the door with Lucy. His tummy did feel a bit odd but he was determined to find Alan and then they would all be grateful and stop treating him like a little boy.

He wondered if Alan had been kidnapped. If so, he'd either be dead or miles away by now. He went through a broken-down gate in the wall at the side of the house and stood looking over the Loch. His mother and Mrs. Macpherson had disappeared into the ravine, among the cluster of bright green larch trees and darker bushes.

He felt even more sure now that Alan would be among those ruins and started to run through the scratchy heather, with Lucy bobbing up and down on her wiry little legs. The rain fell like mist again and he saw a figure ahead. It was a woman, carrying a bundle. He heard her harsh breathing as she ran and she was wearing a strange long dress. Lucy barked and ran forward but the woman ran faster, into the mist.

Lucy barked again as a man burst out of the greyness. There was something dark in his hand. Was it a gun? Tim caught a glimpse of a dirty red coat and then the man was gone, after the woman.

Tim was so scared that he nearly turned back. Lucy stood, puzzled, her small body tense, her long plumed tail tucked between her legs instead of curving over her back. He thought of all the warnings he'd had about strangers. Was the man going to hurt that woman? Ought he to go back and get the Police? He listened for screams, a shot, but heard nothing but the lonely cry of a moorland bird and the distant mewing of seagulls.

Perhaps the man was Alan's kidnapper. At this very moment he was rushing off to make that telephone call, asking for a million pounds in return for Alan. The woman was his accomplice but they'd quarrelled . . .

He forced himself to run on, down the slope as the heather gave way to tough sea-grass and the shingled beach of the Loch and he imagined Mum saying briskly, 'Don't be silly, anyone could see from the Macphersons' house that they couldn't pay a ransom.'

Panting, he kicked irritably at the stones. Why were all his exciting ideas so impractical? Very probably those people were tramps who had fallen out.

Seagulls swooped and birds with long legs and bills

stalked along the beach. Dad would have fun with his bird-book. It was a bit like the seaside but not half as good. The dark green water rippled up to him and he took off one boot and sock to try it. Icy water froze has bare toes. There'd be no bathing here, he thought, as he put his sock on his wet foot.

He could see now that there was a kind of causeway to the island and the ruins. It was covered with water but he could see gleams of white rock, which meant it wasn't deep. Was the tide coming in or going out?

Lucy barked at the water excitedly and chased after a sea-bird as he walked to where he could see the causeway better. The more he stared at the hump of land, the more certain he became that Alan was there. It would be an adventure to find him and just show Becca he could do something on his own. He would have to leave Lucy behind.

'Stay,' he said as he took off his boots and socks.

She sat down with a very sad expression on her round furry face. Her long ears and moustaches of hair drooped.

When he began to walk into the water, he heard her bark and the next minute she was swimming beside him, tiny legs going hard and her long coat floating on either side of her body. With a sigh, he picked her up under one arm. She was light but it would be hard to carry her all the way. Then he looked at the swirling water over the causeway. Was the tide coming in? It was cold and he couldn't swim. Well, he could swim a little with armbands but without them he always kept one toe on the bottom. Becca, of course, was in the swimming team at school and had already dived off the top board at the baths.

The water on the causeway didn't look more than a foot deep. He walked on, from the shingle to the smooth stone bottom. He'd rolled up his jeans but it seemed too cold to take them off. After a few steps he couldn't feel his numb feet. He kept his eyes on the hump of land ahead and tried not to look down at the dark green water on either side of the causeway. Supposing there *was* a monster in the Loch?

It was a mistake not looking because he went too close to the edge and his right leg went down, down, into deep water. He only kept his balance by an effort and nearly dropped Lucy.

His heart pounded as he staggered on, slipping down into the worn humps and dips of the causeway. He felt very lonely. Nobody knew where he was. The rock underneath his feet was slippery and Lucy wriggled. He wanted to go back.

Suddenly, he saw a boy, just ahead, splashing out of the water, up to the island. Was it Alan? He saw bare feet, a ragged rug-thing wrapped round the boy and a wild head of red hair. The sun had fought through the clouds and glinted now on a knife in the boy's hand.

The shock made him stumble and he fell headlong into the icy water lapping the causeway. He heard Lucy's despairing yelp as he dropped her and felt complete panic as the water closed over his head.

19

CHAPTER TWO

His head was under and he swallowed a great mouthful of salty water. He couldn't breathe and thought he was going to die. Then his scrabbling hands hit the causeway and he pulled himself up and found the water only came to his shoulders. The cool wind on his wet shoulders made him shiver violently and the bitter cold of the water drove breath from his body.

Where was Lucy? For a moment he thought she had drowned and then he saw her trying to get on to the causeway, her eyes desperate. He hauled her up. Her long hair clung to her and she seemed to have shrunk but she shook herself and ran to the island.

The hump was bigger than it looked from the shore and shaped a little like a crouching animal, with the ruins where the head might be. There was the remains of an old gate-post here, with a hump of stone on top. Still shaking with cold, he stared at it and realised that the head had gone but it had once been an animal, perhaps another cat.

He followed the broken-down track round the side of the hump of land. His bare feet were still numb with cold, making him stumble. It had stopped raining and there was a strange quietness here, where the grassy mound to his left shielded him from the wind. Below, a short cliff led to rocks, tumbling into the Loch. There were cracks and dark places further along the granite cliff and he wondered if there were caves here.

The track bent to the left and there were the ruins surrounded by rusty barbed wire and a notice, DANGER: KEEP OUT. Great dark stones covered in lichen reared like giants' teeth beyond and at the far end, there was a tower with the top broken off.

Had Alan got through the wire? Lucy barked and Tim heard mewing, like a gull's. Then he saw the cat. It was huge and striped, with a flat head and it ran on, round the edge of the wire. Lucy chased it. The cat disappeared under the wire and Lucy squeezed after it, squeaking as her long wet hair was caught up for a moment.

The rain-soaked grass under the wire here was flattened as if someone had crept underneath. He lay flat and wriggled under, hearing a tearing sound as the wire caught the back of his jeans. There would be trouble, later on. Lucy ran on into a dark archway in the ruined tower.

Tim looked doubtfully at the pile of stones that had already fallen from the tower. The notice had said DANGER. Supposing the whole thing fell over and he was buried alive? He called but Lucy didn't come back.

Was Alan there? He might get hurt if any more stones fell. He imagined the tower falling and himself pulling Alan out just in time. 'It was so brave of you, Tim,' Becca would say and Mrs. Macpherson would hug him and cry and might even give them a free holiday.

All the same, afterwards he had to be honest with himself. He might not have gone into the tower if Lucy hadn't yelped in a muffled way. The thought of tiny Lucy, pancake flat under the stones, drove him on and he ran inside. There was a spiral staircase, going down one way and the other, up to a patch of sky. Lucy barked again and he followed the stairs down. The edges had crumbled away and he dared not hold on to the wall in case that fell too. It smelled of dark, musty tombs and he was very scared. He saw a faint gleam of light as he went round the last spiral and Lucy's barking rose to a fury.

As he neared the bottom, he heard a voice calling, 'Help, I'm stuck!'

He stumbled as the last step crumbled under foot and saw he was in a kind of dungeon, with light shining under a big door. Lucy was scrabbling at it and he saw a fallen stone had blocked the door. 'I'm in here,' said a boy. 'I can't open it. Help!' The voice was hoarse as if the boy had been crying.

As he heaved away at the stone, Tim wished he was big and hefty like Becca. Another might come down, just like this one. Presumably Alan, if it was Alan, had got inside and banging the door had dislodged the stone. Supposing it happened again?

He tugged and pulled. 'Is that Alan in there?' he called breathlessly.

'Yes! Please hurry up,' Alan said.

In the end, Tim found the only way he could move the stone was by lying on the ground, pulling and using his feet as a sort of lever. With a terrific effort he pushed it to one side and a little shower of brickwork fell from the tower above. His heart beat very fast as he thought how dreadful it would be to be smothered underneath and nobody would know. It would be like the nightmares he had when he was younger and woke up at the wrong end of the bed, unable to breathe. He pushed at the door and it suddenly gave way. He almost fell inside on to a boy who was sitting on the ground holding a torch. 'Better get up quickly,' Tim said. 'It doesn't seem safe here.'

22

The boy followed him without a word, Lucy dancing delightedly and licking his legs as they went up the twisting stairs to the light. 'Whatever did you go there for?' Tim said, turning to look at Alan in the daylight. 'You must have been there all day.'

'It's usually all right,' he said crossly. Alan was a tall, thin boy and his freckles stood out like spots on his pale face. His red hair was full of dust from the dungeon and there was a streak of dirt on his nose. 'Thanks for getting me out,' he added grudgingly.

'Let's get back quickly. They're waiting for you,' Tim said. Alan limped badly. 'How did you hurt your leg?' Tim asked.

'It's always like that,' Alan snapped.

Tim remembered the cat. 'That cat—went this way. Wouldn't it get hurt? I mean, if something fell on it.'

Alan looked at him strangely. 'Wildcats can take care of themselves,' he said, as if he didn't like them.

'There's one on your gate-post,' Tim said, remembering.

'It's our clan, Clan Chattan,' Alan said.

'Anyway, you couldn't have been there all day,' Tim said, remembering. 'I saw you ahead of me, when I came over. You must have only just got trapped in that cellar.'

'It wasn't me,' Alan said.

'Then it must have been another boy just like you,' Tim said.

'I came here this morning, wandered about a bit . . . looking . . .' Alan stopped. 'I dug a bit. Then I went into the dungeon. I was stuck there four hours—I looked at my watch. What did the boy look like?'

Tim described him. 'I couldn't see him really well because I fell in,' he said.

'I suppose it was someone from the village,' Alan said.

Tim looked back at the ruins. 'Where is he now?'

'You do go on,' said Alan. 'He's maybe in another part of the ruins, or climbing one of the cliffs.' He looked sideways at Tim, rather as if he didn't like what he saw. 'I suppose you're one of the Carters and that guinea-pig is your dog. I bet she sleeps on your bed at night.'

'Lucy's a Tibetan dog—a Lhasa Apso,' Tim said crossly. She did sleep on his bed but he wasn't going to say so. 'She's very bouncy, for her size—she can walk a long way.' He slowed down a bit as Alan was hobbling so much.

'Do those castle ruins really belong to you?' he asked, trying to be friendly.

Alan grunted.

Tim remembered the ragged man and woman. 'Are there some tramps or something round here?' he asked. 'I saw a funny-looking man chasing a woman down the heather. They wore odd clothes.'

Alan stood still a moment. 'No tramps as far as I know,' he said slowly. 'You shouldn't be out here on your own anyway. You're too young. It's wild country—not your London park.'

Tim could have hit him then. 'I'm eleven,' he said. 'Same age as you, I bet. I can't help being small for my age any more than you . . .' He had nearly said something about Alan's leg. As if Alan had guessed, he wouldn't talk any more and they walked over the causeway—only a few inches under water now—and across the heather.

When they came to the house Lucy barked at Tara, who was outside in the courtyard with Tim's mother, Mrs. Macpherson and a strange man. 'Why are you both so wet?' Alan's mother said. She looked as if she was trying not to seem worried. 'How could you stay out all day like that, Alan?'

'I found him . . .' Tim began. Then suddenly something stopped him saying he'd found Alan in the castle ruins. Maybe he had special reasons for going there. Although Tim didn't like the Scottish boy, it was bad enough not being able to walk properly. 'I found him wandering about. His watch had stopped,' Tim said, feeling clever.

'I can speak for myself,' Alan said rudely.

Mrs. Macpherson introduced Tim to the big man. 'Mr. Wayland Scott,' she said. 'He may be buying our house and grounds.' Alan ran off then with a look of hatred.

Mr. Scott looked after Alan with a worried expression. 'He doesn't like the idea,' he said. 'But I'm trying to persuade Mrs. Macpherson to sell me this beautiful house and grounds to make it into an hotel where people can come and enjoy the scenery. It's in my blood, you know, Scotland. I've always dreamed of buying a place up here and now I have just come to a house further along the Loch. I have a boat, renamed it *Wildcat*—you must all come out in it. I believe some of my ancestors fought on the side of the English when the Scots tried to put their Prince Charles on the throne, couple of hundred years ago. I expect you'll forgive me that, though!' He laughed and flashed his white teeth at them before getting into a brand new Rolls and driving off.

Dad and Becca passed him, in the old car. There was an argument when they both arrived because Becca was cross with Tim for finding Alan. 'Well, you didn't *really* find him, did you?' she said nastily. 'I mean, you said he was wandering about. I expect he was coming back anyway.'

Tim was sent upstairs to change 'and you've torn the back of your jeans, on the very first day,' Mum said crossly.

When he came down, he heard Mrs. Macpherson talking to Alan. 'You're never to go off like that again,' she said. 'After all, these guests have only just arrived and they're tired with their journey—they didn't want to start looking for you.'

'I didn't ask them to,' Alan said.

She looked furious and Tim could see she was just stopping herself from saying something really angry, because he was there. Alan went out with Tara and Lucy tried to follow but Tim held her. Lucy had some idea that she wasn't a very small dog at all and also, that all dogs, however large, would love her.

'What a weird sort of boy,' Becca said later when they were having cocoa in the kitchen.

Mrs. Macpherson and Alan had gone to milk the one cow, not the herd Dad had imagined, and fetch the eggs. Mum was upstairs, carefully hanging up the clothes in her tidy way and probably ticking off her list. Dad had gone for a stroll down to the Loch. Becca wanted to go too but Mum said they ought to have an early night after the journey.

'Fancy lumping me with you,' Becca said. 'I'm not tired. After all, I'm nearly a teenager, not a child. I don't think that Alan likes us being here, do you? He won't talk to me. It's going to be dead boring here except for swimming and walking. Pity we aren't allowed to that island place—it looks interesting.'

Tim felt his ears burn but Becca didn't see. When she talked she flowed on and didn't notice if anyone was listening or not. 'And I'd like to go out with that man in his boat.'

Tim lay in bed that night thinking of those strange people running over the heather and of the boy with the knife and wondering where he had gone. And where did that cat live? Maybe it was because he had been thinking about cats but as he went to sleep in the huge, damp-smelling bedroom there was a strange howling outside. It sounded as if some big animal—bigger than a cat—was pacing round outside. He shivered. The house was so old and creaky. Supposing there was some animal creeping through the window . . .

The next morning everything seemed normal. They ate porridge and eggs and bacon. Dad went on about the porridge as if it were a rare food. 'Absolutely delicious and so Scottish,' he said.

'Did you hear a sort of howling in the night?' Tim asked Alan, determined to make him speak.

'No,' the boy said.

'Are there any wolves in Scotland?' Tim asked and was cross when everyone laughed.

Dad said, 'A hundred years ago there were wild boars, wolves and of course the wildcats we have now.'

'I expect it was a wildcat,' said Mrs. Macpherson.

She looked thoughtful as she began to wash up. 'My husband used to say there was a legend attached to this house. Something to do with the 1745 Rebellion. I'm a Macdonald myself and my husband's clan and mine used to be at each other's throats in the past.'

Tim imagined great hairy Scotsmen, leaping with bared teeth to bite each other's throats out like wolves.

'Some people have seen a ghost from the past here—the English plundered and burnt the house after the battle of Culloden,' said Mrs. Macpherson. Tim lost interest a little—it sounded too much like history at school.

Mum offered to shop for Mrs. Macpherson while Dad mended the car and Becca went with her. Tim said he would help his father, which wasn't quite true. He was what Dad called 'hack-handed' but he liked being with his father. At home, Tim escaped from Becca and her giggling friends to Dad's allotment. Then he could sit in the little shed and read. He and his father would drink tea out of a thermos in the companionable earthy gloom.

Tim mooched about thinking he would look at the tumbledown side of the house and see if a mad aunt or a pale child came to the window.

The old stables formed one side of the yard, and on the other, by the ruined side of the house, was a wall with an open gate, through which he could see a kitchen-garden. He wandered in. A few fat clouds floated in the sky but the morning sun was hot in the walled plot. Bees buzzed in the red flowers of the runner beans and he felt happy. The strange events of yesterday evening seemed remote here. He and Lucy sat by a row of bolting lettuces and stared up at the house.

He was just imagining himself rescuing the pale child when he saw something moving. There was a white face at the window! It disappeared so quickly that he wondered if he could have imagined it. He stared until his eyes felt hot but nothing else moved there.

Alan and Tara came into the kitchen garden. Alan was carrying a hoe and he frowned at Tim.

'Don't you want to go out?' he asked.

'No—I'm exploring a bit,' Tim said. He was determined not to be squashed.

Alan grunted and began to hoe a weedy patch of carrots.

'Couldn't you show me the shut-up part of the house?' Tim asked him. If Alan looked furtive, then perhaps there was someone kept prisoner there.

'No,' Alan said. He looked at Tim with his slanting green cat's eyes. 'After my father died, there was a storm and part of the chimney crashed through the roof so it's not safe there.'

Tim was sure now that the pale child was locked up. Perhaps he was a batty cousin or an invalid ... Alan's hunched shoulders looked so unfriendly that Tim went out of another door at the far end of the kitchen-garden with Lucy. She trotted ahead of him, her tail corkscrewing over her back and down in a cascade of black and white hair. They went past a big hen-run and then down a narrow path between sharp-smelling nettles and a tangle of brambles. Tim's legs were stung and he might have turned back only Lucy bounced on and wouldn't stop. The path led through a prickly hawthorn thicket and the remains of an old yew hedge.

After a while he found himself in a small clearing,

surrounded by old ragged yews and weeds. It was a graveyard. There were small headstones, covered in green moss and lichen and feathery grasses ran riot.

It was very quiet. Tim's heart beat fast. This must be where all the dead Macphersons were buried. He looked closely at one of the tilting stones and scratched away at the moss until he could read the letters. ANGUS 1906 – 1916. The boy had only been a year younger than Tim.

Suddenly he felt trapped in this strange place. He called Lucy but she sprang off and jumped onto the next grave, looking back defiantly at him. He put out his hand and grabbed at her collar and then saw the cat's head carved on the tombstone and the blob on top, which looked rather like the cat on the gate-post. He scratched at the lichen again and just made out the date and part of the name: C . . U . . Y. 1740 – 1746. This family must have had a great many sickly children. Perhaps this was a child's graveyard.

A rook startled him, screaming loudly and he grabbed Lucy and went out at the far end of the graveyard, pushing through a gap. He walked through tall sleepy-scented cowparsley and came out by a collapsing stone wall.

A gust of wind hit his cheek, just as if someone was passing him and, for a moment, he thought he saw two dim figures, a woman and a boy, running through the gap in the wall and over the heather. Then he blinked and they had gone. They must be running the other way, to his right and hidden by the wall. He felt a bit strange and decided to go back. He was just passing the hen-run when he met Alan's mother. She was carrying a bucket. 'Exploring?' she asked with a smile. 'Like to help me find eggs?'

The thought came to him that he had a chance now. If he hurried he might find the key to that empty part of the house while she was gone. 'Thanks—must get back now,' he said and hurried on.

Dad's feet stuck out from the car as Tim went past. He stood in the big hall, staring at the locked door and thinking. At home, the keys hung on a hook in the kitchen, neatly labelled by Mum. He went into the kitchen and looked all round. He found a cork noticeboard by the sink; a notice saying *Carters July 16th* was pinned to it and on a hook beneath, hung keys, some labelled. He took the one with *House: hall door* on it.

His hand shook a little as he put the big key in the lock of the panelled door and he was surprised when it turned easily, as if it had often been used. He went over the bare boards of the hall beyond and up the shallow, dusty stairs, with Lucy following. A gust of wind from upstairs swung the door to with a heavy thud. Supposing he couldn't open it again?

He knew he was being silly but he was both nervous and excited at the thought of meeting the pale child. Lucy's claws clattered in the silence and he called her as she bounded ahead. He found her on the landing above, peering into a jagged hole. Above was another hole in the roof, covered with polythene. He put out his hand to catch her but Lucy skittered round the hole and went to sniff at a closed door. She must have heard the pale child moving about!

His heart beating fast, he forced himself to turn the carved wooden doorhandle . . .

CHAPTER THREE

Tim and Lucy went into the room. It was dim and panelled with one window and tattered curtains. There was an old bed, a broken chair and a desk. There was no pale child cowering in a corner. Perhaps she was in another room. She would have heard them come upstairs —wouldn't she call out?

He looked at the open book on the desk. Beside it was a coke can and a half-eaten scone marked the page. So someone did come in here! He looked through the window and saw the kitchen-garden and the place where he had sat, looking up. Alan was no longer hoeing.

The book was some kind of Scottish history. He moved the scone and read:

'After the battle of Culloden, when Ian Macpherson was slain, his wife, Catherine, pursued by English soldiers and Highland levies, managed to bury the family silver and jewels. Her son Alan died in a fight with a soldier, it is thought, but his body was never found. The family legend is that he defended himself with a jewelled dirk which had been in the family for some time. It was reputed to keep the Macphersons of Archnacross from all evil. This branch of the family has suffered misfortunes since that time and it is said that when the dirk is found, they will be happy again. English soldiers set fire to the house and orchard and . . .'

Lucy barked and Tim turned round to see Alan's angry face. Tara stood beside him, loftily ignoring Lucy.

'This is my room,' he said. He grabbed Tim's arm and jerked him away.

Surprise made Tim push Alan back and then the bigger boy's fist shot forward but Tim dodged. 'You're just a bully!' he shouted, hitting out. In a minute they were wrestling together and Lucy squealed as someone stood on her tail. Alan pushed Tim towards the window. He glanced round, and saw fire. The kitchen-garden had gone and there was an orchard whose trees were in flames, flames that consumed the pinky-white blossom and nearly hid the woman running with a bundle in her hand.

'Fire!' Tim cried out. 'The trees are on fire.'

'Trying to trick me?' Alan said, but he stopped pushing. He looked. 'There's no fire.' Mrs. Macpherson was walking through the sunlit kitchen-garden with a bucket of eggs.

'There was an orchard, on fire,' he said. 'And someone running.'

'You made it up. That's in the book,' Alan said sharply.

It was as if he hoped Tim *was* making it up. If he wasn't, how could they both bear the knowledge of another world touching theirs? It was one thing to enjoy a ghost story but quite another to see a ghost yourself.

'There's no such things as ghosts,' Tim said, quoting Mum, who only believed what she saw. 'Why did you hit me? Why didn't you want me to see this room? You hate us for coming here, don't you?'

32

Alan sat on the desk, fiddling with the half-eaten scone and breaking it into pieces. 'It's my place,' Alan said. 'This room was mine once. Then the storm came and the chimney fell . . . I don't really hate you at all but I don't like our having visitors paying to stay with us. And now we have to leave. Look at that picture.'

Tim hadn't really noticed the picture hanging above the fireplace. It was a boy with red hair and green eyes like Alan's. He wore plaid over his shoulder and held a short silvery sword in one hand. Under the picture was a tattered old banner, torn and singed at the edges. There was a cat, standing on its hind legs and snarling and the words, TOUCH NOT THE CAT BUT A GLOVE.

'That was another Alan Macpherson,' Alan said. 'He lived here and that is our family motto.'

'But if you don't have lodgers and you don't sell the house, how is your mother going to manage?' Tim asked. 'It costs a lot to eat nowadays.' He was quoting Mum, who was always hunting after supermarket bargains.

Alan suddenly grasped his shoulders hard. 'Promise you won't tell . . .'

'OK, I promise,' Tim said.

'I'm going to find the dirk and the lost silver and jewels.'

'So that's what you were doing when I found you yesterday,' Tim said excitedly.

At that moment, they heard Mrs. Macpherson's voice calling 'Alan, Alan,' from the yard.

'We'll have to get out,' Alan said. 'After yesterday, she'll be mad if I stay up here and I've left the hoeing half done.'

Tara barked and Lucy began to whine. 'Muffle that guinea-pig of yours,' Alan said.

'She's not,' Tim said indignantly but he picked Lucy up and he followed Alan past the gaping hole in the floor, down a mushroom-smelling corridor and dim, narrow dusty backstairs.

33

Lucy grew heavier as Alan switched on a light and went into a huge cellar. Tim jumped as a bit of plaster hit his shoulder and some of the cellar ceiling showered down. It seemed almost as crumbly as the castle tower. There were more stone steps leading up to a closed door. 'Kitchen,' Alan explained, 'but she bolts it.'

The dog struggled so Tim put her down. She scrambled with them after Alan, over a load of coke and up a slithery black coal chute. Tim felt his knee go through his jeans. Then Alan pushed at a rotting flap door and they were out, in the middle of a nettlebed.

'I've only gone this way once before,' Alan panted as they stood up. Lucy pushed through the flap, a small grey and black dog now.

'How do we explain the coal away?' Tim asked.

Alan laughed and wiped his coally hand across his nose.

'Now you've got a black face too,' Tim said.

Sweet-smelling elders surrounded them and through the greenery he could see the Loch, blue and harmless today in the sun. They did their best with spit and bits of grass and then ran to the kitchen door. Alan's mother and Dad were drinking coffee together and looked rather startled at the coally boys.

'Where have you been, Alan?' his mother asked. 'And you're filthy! I wish you'd learn to finish a job. You know I wanted that hoeing done before the weeds got too much. I thought while you were on holiday, I'd get extra help.'

'Sorry,' he said. 'But it's so boring.'

'I'll help you,' Tim said. Alan was the only person who knew he had seen ghosts and Tim felt a kind of bond with him. He was in a happy dream that he had found the silver and jewels and saved the Macphersons' home when he realised Dad had been talking. 'What did you say?' he asked.

'I said I saw a buzzard while I was doing the car,' Dad said. 'It was hovering, then it swooped down. Lovely!'

His eyes glinted behind his glasses. 'We could go off bird-watching all the afternoon.' Typically Dad, he had forgotten all about his idea of helping with the small-holding. Sometimes, Tim thought Dad seemed like a younger brother. 'And the car runs now,' he said proudly.

The boys washed, then went to the kitchen garden. On the way, Alan nudged Tim and he hooked the key back quickly.

'You don't have to help,' Alan said in his normal grumpy voice.

'If I do, can I come and look for the treasure too?' Tim asked.

'I suppose so,' Alan said without much enthusiasm. 'Though I don't know where to look next.'

He gave Tim the job of picking up the weeds and putting them in the barrow. Tim kept looking up, wondering if he would see the flaming orchard again but soon, he was so hot and bored that the uneasy feeling went. He wondered about the treasure. 'Was that castle lived in when the treasure was hidden?' he asked.

Alan leaned on his hoe. Sweat was trickling down his face. 'The old father lived there and he died in the fire,' he said. 'There was never enough money to rebuild the castle so nobody has lived there since.'

Tim thought. 'Well, how could she have hidden the treasure there if it was on fire?'

'Before,' Alan said, going back to his hoeing.

Tim thought again of the woman running through the flaming orchard, carrying the bundle.

'The old man, the grandfather—another Alan Macpherson—got his servants to shoot at the English with a cannon, from the castle. They might have left it alone but they got so angry they burned that too, as well as the house.'

'Did he get out?' Tim asked.

'No,' said Alan.

Tim imagined the old man, coughing, shouting and then the roar of flames and he was burning like the guy on their bonfire last year. He tried to throw off the feeling of horror by getting at Alan. 'What's that stupid saying on your wall, TOUCH NOT THE CAT BUT A GLOVE? It doesn't mean anything.'

Alan's eyes narrowed. 'It's not stupid, you Sassenach!' he shouted. 'It's our family motto, as I told you. It means, don't touch the cat, that's the wildcat, without a glove. It's the fiercest animal in Great Britain!' He was waving his hoe by then and Tim backed away. He dodged and ran off to the house. Alan was nothing but a show-off.

Mum arrived back then, with shopping and news that she had met Mr. Scott and his daughter and he had asked them out in his boat that afternoon. His daughter had just arrived last night from America. 'He asked all of us,' Mum said, looking at Mrs. Macpherson and Alan as they all ate bread and cheese and oatcakes round the kitchen table.

'I've got work to do,' Alan said.

'You've finished the hoeing, why not go?' said his mother. 'I must cook the dinner.'

Alan shook his head.

'Lovely,' Dad said happily. 'I might see an oystercatcher or a cormorant.'

'I suppose Tim's going to say he's got tummy-ache,' Becca said nastily.

He wished he could punch her, hard. 'I'm not coming. I want to explore. And I'll help Alan.'

'Oh well, that girl looks more fun than my boring brother,' Becca said.

Tim threw an oatcake at her and got into more trouble. When they had gone, Alan said he had to clean the henhouse.

Tim hadn't really intended doing any more work—he thought Alan would start treasure-hunting right away. He began to wish he had gone with the others as he helped

36

clean out the run. It was hot and smelly and flies buzzed round his head. Hens kept coming back and putting anxious heads through their door and each time Lucy's motherly heart delighted at the sight of large feathered puppies, wagged her tail and tried to lick them, the hen would rush off with an affronted squawk. Tara lay aloof, in the sun.

'Can't we stop now and hunt for the treasure?' Tim asked. Alan was putting clean straw in the nest boxes.

'You sound like a bairn,' he said scornfully. 'It's not just a game, finding the treasure. How'd you like to live in a poky place in Inverness instead of here?'

Tim lived in a poky house in town anyway and he felt at the moment that it would be much better than a fly-ridden henhouse in the country. 'I know it's not a game,' he said. 'Have you searched systematically?' Mum always said things like that to Dad when he lost something, which was often.

'You use long words, don't you?' Alan said. 'Well, it could be anywhere. I've been searching all over since I found the book, and since Mum said we'd have to sell.'

'What about that sword thing, that brings you luck?' Tim asked.

'The dirk,' said Alan. 'I thought it would be with the treasure.' He scattered sawdust on the floor. 'Or if the boy died fighting near the fire, he might have got burned so the dirk could have lain in the long grass or under a stone all this time.' He looked round the henhouse. 'I thought I'd try by the burn. Let's go.'

The dogs forgot their sleepiness and bounced through the heather. Tara bayed, deep in her throat and a small herd of red deer bounded out of the ravine and up the opposite hill-side. Lucy barked sharply and Alan called the dogs to heel. The deer were led by an immense stag with many-branched antlers and the fawns sprang behind their mothers on legs so thin that they looked as if they might snap.

The ravine was bigger than it looked from above. They walked under ancient, twisted trees, hung with pale green lichen and darker green moss and a great rushing sound filled the insect-humming air.

Tim slapped at the midges and felt prickles where they had bitten his neck. He remembered Mum packing anti-midge cream in her box and wished he had put it on.

The stubby, half-dead trees were mixed with paintbox green larches and dark little firs. They walked softly on pine needles. It was like the poem he had read at school . . . 'and no birds sang'. He felt that other world of the past was very near to him and he shivered.

The white froth of the burn glinted through the dark trees and he followed Alan to the edge of the ravine. It surprised him how fast and deep the water was as it creamed over rocks from the steep hillside to their left, rushing into a black hole in a bridge of rock.

'We ought to have brought a spade,' Alan said. 'Above that hole where the water goes would be a good place. I've got a penknife.' They walked along the narrow path above the river. Tara and Lucy trotted ahead, enjoying themselves.

It was then that Tim saw the woman again, standing on the bridge of mossy rock and looking back tensely, as if she were listening. He looked back too and saw the dark shapes of men and the glint of guns.

There was a terrific bang which echoed through the ravine.

CHAPTER FOUR

'She's shot!' Tim cried in horror, looking away. He felt sick, thinking of the woman lying bleeding.

'It's a wildcat,' Alan was saying as the noise of the gunshot died away. Lucy barked wildly and Tara ran back along the path. A big striped cat with a bushy tail was limping away from the bridge of rock into the bushes.

There was a confusion of barking and a man called out, 'Get your dog off!' Alan and Tim ran back down the path and found Tara standing over a man on the ground. A gun lay by his side. Lucy ran forward. Confused as to whether he was friend or enemy, she started to lick the man's face, which made him call out even louder and add some Scottish-sounding swear words.

Alan called Tara off and the man got up. He was stocky and his face was weathered and lined like a piece of old wood. 'If your dog hadna pushed me over I'd ha'a second shot at that bloody cat,' he said.

'You're on our land, Mr. Campbell,' Alan said coldly. 'Mr. Scott's land is the other side of the burn.'

'You wait till that creature kills hens,' Mr. Campbell went on. 'It's been at my grouse. She's feeding kits. That's why she's out in the daytime. I'll kill those little beasties if I find them.'

'I think you might have hit the wildcat,' Alan said. 'It was limping a bit.'

'Yes, and you've stopped me putting the creature out of its misery,' Mr. Campbell said. 'Limping about—you know what that's like, Alan Macpherson.'

Alan turned at once and hobbled off towards the rocky bridge where the cat had disappeared.

Tim and the dogs followed, up to the rock and down the narrow path which led from the top of the rock. Tim pushed through tangled Old Man's Beard and found Alan, standing above a full flow of swift dark water which ran into the stillness of the Black Loch. Along the beach was the causeway and further out they saw the big motor yacht sailing from what must be Mr. Scott's house, on the next headland. Alan still did not speak.

Tim knew he was angry but he had to ask him. 'Did you see the woman?' he burst out. 'She sort of turned into the wildcat. And soldiers . . .' He tailed off.

'I just saw the cat,' Alan said in a dull voice. 'And it's got right away, wounded, That gillie's no right to shoot on our land. It's Mr. Scott's the other side of the burn. If it's necessary, I will kill the cat myself. I dinna like the creatures.' He spat the words out and sounded so Scottish that Tim had a job to understand him.

'The treasure might be there, after all,' Tim said, imagining the woman falling, shot, over the place where she had hidden it.

Tim saw Mum, in the bows of the boat, turning to Dad and they both waved. Mr. Scott, wearing a white cap with a peak, was at the helm.

'Hope he falls in and drowns,' Alan said, leading the way back to the rock.

They searched and Alan tried to dig with his penknife. It was mostly rock, even under the grasses, and all they found was a splodge of blood where the cat had been shot. Even Tim could see it was a hopeless task. You would need a proper digger to find anything at all and then you might miss it.

'I've thought of somewhere obvious,' Alan said at last. 'Come on.'

'Could ghosts come back to help us?' Tim asked as they panted up the hill.

'Maybe,' Alan said slowly. 'I've thought they might be like a sort of photograph from the past, printed on the air . . .'

'Or perhaps like TV,' Tim said. 'Sending pictures of themselves through space from . . . ' He hesitated.

'From where?' Alan said.

Tim wasn't sure.

'Well, I never see my father,' Alan said. 'And I'd have thought he'd have wanted to help us. If you have seen ghosts from the past, why haven't you seen *newer* ghosts like my dad?'

'Don't know,' Tim said. Thinking of real ghosts made him feel strange, like the time when Granny died so suddenly—one day talking to them and next gone, like a leaf in the wind. Then, and now, he wanted to go back to the time when life was safe and ordinary.

Alan stopped when they were just inside the garden wall and stared at an old well-head, half buried in tangled honeysuckle and briars.

'There,' he said. 'She could have put the treasure there— Mum said it was very old. We'll just get the cover off.'

It seemed welded on with weeds. Alan scrabbled away at them and Lucy tried to help while Tara lay in the shade. Tim helped Alan tug at the rusty ring of the cover. He was

41

so thirsty and tired. He wanted to give up and come back later as he could hear Mum calling but Alan went on tugging. Tim was afraid he might be thought a wimp if he stopped now. 'You hold round my waist while I pull,' Alan said.

The lid came up so suddenly that Tim fell backwards, pulling Alan with him.

They both untangled themselves and peered inside. 'Can't see any water,' Tim said. The well smelled of slime and something long dead.

'There's something sticking out of one side further down,' Alan said, lying on his stomach. 'I'm going to climb down. Dad said it was dry in the summer and there are lots of cracks in the brickwork for holds.'

He launched himself over the edge before Tim could stop him.

Alan's fingers clung to the top of the well and then he moved further down so Tim could just see the top of his red head. Suddenly he stopped and fell with a yell. He would be killed! Tim looked over fearfully. 'I'll get help,' he called. 'Are you hurt?'

Alan's voice was shaken and muffled. 'I'm all right. Fell on something horribly soft and squidgy. I'm just jolted. And it's not the treasure in that crack, just a sort of plant growing on the side. But I'm going to look in the squidge just in case . . . ugh, what a pong! Better fetch a rope, I suppose.'

Tim found them in the kitchen. Mr. Scott and his daughter were there too. They all came running and Dad brought a rope from the back of his car. He tied it round his waist and threw it to Alan. It was like some strange dance: Mr. Scott held on to Dad and Mrs. Macpherson, Tim and the strange girl helped him pull the rope. Mum and Becca somehow grabbed a bit of Mr. Scott and they all leaned back as Alan climbed up the well.

They must have leaned too far because suddenly they

were in a tangled heap on top of one another with the dogs barking excitedly! Alan lay, panting and dirty on the side of the well. 'I'd have managed only my beastly leg gave way,' he gasped.

'What on earth did you think you were doing?' his mother shouted at him. She had gone very pale.

'Just climbing down,' Alan said.

They all went back to the house while Mrs. Macpherson told Alan he was an idiot and had no sense and he might have broken his good leg and . . .

'All's well now,' Mr. Scott said placidly.

Alan's mother fetched home-made lemonade from the fridge. Tim thought he had never felt so thirsty before.

'What were you looking for?' the strange girl asked him.

'This is Sam,' Mr. Scott said proudly. 'She would come out today, though she's tired from the flight yesterday. Sorry you didn't come out with us, boys. We saw you playing on the Loch shore.'

Playing! Tim knew Alan was as cross as he felt. Sam's wet dark hair was shorter than Alan's and she wore jeans and a bright blue tee-shirt with TEXAS TURKEY on the front and a picture of an armadillo. 'Well, what kind of game was it in the well?' she asked, giggling.

Alan just gave her a scornful look.

'We swam,' Becca said, shaking her own wet hair. 'Dived off the boat,' she said in her usual, show-off way. 'It was icy cold but Sam and I had a race and warmed up.'

'It's a beautiful boat, Tim,' Mum said. 'You really should have come with us.' Her face was rosy. 'We had a glass of wine.'

'And we had masses of coke and cookies. You don't say biscuits in America,' Becca explained.

Tim could see she had made one of her instant friendships. Well, he didn't care. Sam looked really pushy and know-all and he could see that Alan didn't like her.

'*Wildcat*'s a real good boat,' Mr. Scott said happily. 'And I'm just longing to see the real thing. I've read there are some in these parts.'

'Your gillie, Campbell, is trying to kill them,' Alan said. 'He wounded one this afternoon. Says they're taking the grouse.'

Mr. Scott frowned. 'I'll speak to him. I inherited Mr. Campbell when I bought my house and my bit of grouse moor. I think he feels I'm a real foreigner.'

You are, Tim thought. All that smarmy gushing and boasting. Nobody English *or* Scottish would do that.

Dad looked up eagerly. 'I should so love to see one myself! Did you know that they turned white in winter like the ptarmigan and hares? Protective colouring. Was it a big one, Tim? I hope the poor thing wasn't badly wounded.'

'It was big,' Tim said, dreamily staring into the distance. Again he saw the woman and the cat, both fallen.

Alan was sent off to wash the well-slime off, Mrs. Macpherson made tea and the Americans praised her for the oatcakes, scones and shortbread. Tim wished they would go. He had a half-formed plan in his head but he would have to do it alone, which was scaring.

Suddenly Sam fell asleep at the table. 'Jet-lag' said Mr. Scott, carrying her off, and Alan went to milk the cow. Tim followed him. Although Alan had been more friendly, he didn't seem specially pleased to have company. He was a funny friend to have, Tim thought.

Flora was a Jersey cow with big dark eyes. Tim tried milking but only a tiny squirt came out of her teat. Alan laughed. 'You'd never make a country boy,' he said.

Becca looked over the cowshed door. 'So that's where you both are,' she said. 'And were you searching for treasure down the well, Alan? Both been reading too many comics?'

'No,' Tim muttered, again wanting to hit her.

'Mum says you've got to come right away,' Becca said bossily.

He followed her reluctantly.

'Can't think why you like that weird boy,' she said. 'Sam's much more fun. She's been staying on a real ranch like on *Dallas* and she can ride and you should see her swim. She does a proper crawl and that boat must have cost thousands of pounds.'

'That's why you like the Scotts,' Tim said. 'They're rich. Alan's not weird and I like him.' He wondered if he really did.

'And what was he doing down the well?' she said again.

'Oh, shut up!' Tim said.

Becca gave him a push which took him by surprise and he landed in a small prickly bush. He heard Becca laughing behind him as he ran indoors. 'I wish you'd made me an only child,' he shouted to Mum.

She smiled. 'That would be difficult as Becca was born first. But do stop quarrelling. Becca, have you been picking on him?'

'Tell-tale,' Becca said.

Mrs. Macpherson was whipping something in a bowl and pretending not to listen. Dad put down his bird book. 'Come on, both of you. We'll go out on the hill for a walk. The Macphersons have plenty to do.'

Dad hardly ever gave them an order but when he did, they obeyed. Mum fetched the anti-midge cream and they put it on, remembering the bites they'd had already.

Out on the heather behind the house, Becca bounced on ahead, her sturdy legs striding easily over the rough ground. Lucy panted as she jumped up and down over the heather, like a small boat in a rough sea. It was hard work for her and suddenly she sat down, refusing to go on. Tim was tired too and bored because he wanted to be treasure-hunting. He looked back down the hill.

45

He saw the tiny figure of Alan, spade over his shoulder, walking out of the back gate and going down, towards the shore of the Black Loch. So he was going to dig for treasure on his own! Tim was hurt. He could have waited.

Smoke blurred the view . . . beyond the house was the flaming orchard, and running through the fiery trees the dark shape of the woman, coming out from behind a big black barrel. She went on, through the gate at the far end and he saw the top of her head as she went down a clipped yew walk where he had forced his way through weeds, to the little graveyard.

Guns glinted as those other dark shapes surged into the orchard. Then they stopped, as if they had lost the woman, and ran back, across the courtyard and out through a gate in a high wall to the foot of this hill! They were coming straight towards him!

Mum was calling. 'Come on, or you'll miss the sunset . . .'

He stared. The soldiers had gone and the setting sun shone like fire on the windows of the house. The orchard had gone and he saw Mrs. Macpherson, bending to pick a bolting lettuce.

'You look as though you'd seen a ghost,' Dad said when Tim caught up, Lucy bouncing beside him as if she'd never been tired.

'Just puffed,' he said. He felt cold. Up here, with the others, he almost wondered if he had imagined the ghosts. Each time it was like this, as he slipped from one world to another. He thought of that Mrs. Macpherson of long ago. She wouldn't have had time to dig a hole. Alan was wrong to take a spade. She would have had to find a deep crack or cave for her bundle.

'Look, there's grumpy old Alan,' Becca said, pointing.

Alan was digging on the Loch beach, just before the causeway. He was quite near the place where the burn flowed out from the rock. What a silly place to try! Tim thought he might as well be looking for a needle in a haystack.

Dad smiled happily. 'It's so dramatic, the dark Loch with the sun setting,' he said. 'And there's the sea, right beyond the other side of the Loch.'

'You and your "dramatic", Ben,' Mum said, laughing. 'All I can say is, I'm glad of the midge cream up here.'

'Expedition to the sea tomorrow,' Dad said.

Tim was wondering how he could get out of it when he saw two people ahead, silhouetted on the ridge. For a moment, his heart thudded, thinking of the ghosts.

'Hikers,' Dad said and as they approached Tim saw they wore big back-packs. 'Lovely evening,' said the bearded man. His wife smiled at Lucy, who lay on her back, hoping to be tickled.

They went on, down the hill. 'There's a camping place near Mr. Scott's house,' Mum said.

Tim felt cross at the thought of campers. Here the moor, the burn and the Black Loch ruled supreme. There was no need for people. He knew how Alan felt. And if the house became a proper hotel there would be people all over the moor and a car park and maybe places for snacks . . . No, he *had* to find the treasure.

CHAPTER FIVE

'That was really superb,' Dad said, putting down his knife and fork with a sigh.

'Brill,' said Becca. She had eaten two helpings.

'Very tender,' said Mum.

'It was one of our own hens,' said Mrs. Macpherson.

Tim hadn't eaten very much and now he was glad. He didn't like the thought of one of those bustling, anxious hens dying for his supper. Alan had come in late, dirty and cross. He seemed to have gone back into his shell again and didn't want to talk to Tim.

Luckily everyone became hooked on to a TV thriller after supper so he said he was tired. Alan was out, shutting up the hens, and Mrs. Macpherson making coffee so he was able to slide out, with Lucy at his heels.

Bats squealed in the dusk. In the kitchen-garden the bean-poles were dark against the paler stone of the wall and the beanstalks grew round them like dark, writhing snakes. Although it was still warm, he shivered, thinking of the woman running and the trees on fire, long ago. Once he had been ambushed and chased down the road by a gang from school and he remembered the panic as they drew near, waving sticks.

Nothing happened. The kitchen-garden was quietly secret. When he heard Alan calling Tara from the direction of the hen-run, Tim decided to avoid him. He went out of the walled garden and down the side of the house to the gate leading to the moor, where he ran over the rough ground in the green dusk. One star shone and a misty moon was rising, throwing tiny shadows from each clump of heather. Lucy whined uneasily and kept close to his heels, her bushy tail drooping. She was scared of the creatures of the night.

He felt lonely and looked back. A light shone through the kitchen window and he saw a dark figure moving. Perhaps there would be shortbread with the coffee. He wanted to go back and forget all about ghosts. Then he realised this was exactly what Becca would expect him to do—give up—so he went on down the track through the heather towards the Loch. What was that dark shape crouched by the outpouring of the burn? 'We might see a monster,' he remembered Becca saying.

Lucy barked and he saw the shadowy forms of two people ahead. 'Out late,' said the camping man.

'Pop in for cocoa on your way back if you want,' said the woman. 'There's our tent.' She pointed to the dark humped shape.

They strode on, talking and laughing. Before they were out of sight, Lucy whined and Tim saw the ghost woman running with the boy towards the ravine. A tattered-looking soldier ran just past Tim, who could see the gun at his belt and smell his sweat. Surely ghosts didn't smell?

The woman and the boy ran straight through the campers, who did not stop talking, and the soldier ran after them. Lucy growled and came running back to Tim with her tail hanging low. Tim's legs felt weak and he sat down. He ought to be used to the ghosts but he was not. Supposing they became stronger, so he saw them all the time? Supposing they became more real than the people round him and drew him back into the past?

Lucy pressed her warmth close to him for comfort. He tried to work it out. Why should it be only himself and Lucy who had seen the ghosts? Perhaps they came to him for a purpose, so he could find the silver. But why hadn't they appeared to Alan or to Mrs. Macpherson? Did he have a special gift for ghosts? He remembered the boy again—over the causeway—when he had thought it was a friend of Alan's—or Alan himself. The dirk had flashed in the air. If he found the dirk the good fortune would follow. The campers called out to him but he took no notice and ran on, towards the causeway.

It was bare of water but slippery and lonely. He looked back and saw the campers had lit a little stove which looked friendly and he wished he had stayed for cocoa after all. Even the ghost boy would be company here.

Lucy nudged his leg and he felt better. He scrambled up from the causeway and saw an old coke can, shining in the moon. Ordinary people had come over here and left ordinary litter and this made him feel better.

He chose the same cliff path as before, to the right of the castle hump. His foot slipped once and he realised that the cliff was at least twenty feet above jagged-looking rocks. Where there were rocks, there were caves. He walked on, past the place where he had scrambled through the wire to the castle, and here was the end of the promontory, with the moon silvering the sea.

Lucy whined and ran ahead. Suddenly the white plume of her tail disappeared and he heard her squeak and scrabble. He ran forward and was in time to see her slither down a little steep path leading to a small cove, just above water-level. She did not come back when he called but slithered to the bottom and ran across the flat wet rock. He slid and scrambled after her and he was reaching for her collar when she whined and looked up at one of the caves in the black-rock cliffs. The moon showed the dark gap, nearly half-way up.

It was then that he saw the eyes shining above in the darkness of the cave, glittering in the moonlight!

CHAPTER SIX

Tim was exhausted by the time he had gone back over the causeway. It had been hard to get up the little cliff path, pushing Lucy in front of him and he had been so frightened. How silly he had been to run away like that. He told himself firmly that it must have been some animal, living on the cliffs.

'Tim!' Becca ran forward with the campers behind her. 'We were coming to look for you. It's far too dark to be out so late on your own. What have you been doing? I slipped out when I couldn't find you. Mum and Dad haven't noticed yet that you aren't there. They think you're in your room.'

'Better get your little brother home right away,' said the woman, in a yukky voice.

'What were you doing, little brother?' Becca asked as they panted up the heather towards the house, the moon casting their shadows long in front of them.

'Mind your own business and don't call me little,' he

shouted, giving her a push. She stepped sideways and trod on Lucy's tail, making her squeak.

'I'll find out,' Becca shouted back. 'I could tell on you to Mum and Dad. They'd explode if they knew you'd been to those ruins again and at night.'

'You're a nerk, a nurd, a tell-tale rat!' he yelled. The sound seemed to echo round the hills. 'You're a big fat bully and I've always hated you and I shan't tell where I've been whatever you do.'

'Shut up, you wimpy weakly fish-face!' Becca screeched as she ran past him to the house.

Mum met him at the kitchen door. 'We only just found you were out,' she said. 'I thought you had gone to bed. Becca says you've been to the castle ruins. Really, Tim, Mrs. Macpherson said they were dangerous ...' She rattled on, angrily.

They all fussed round him as if he were a baby, giving him cocoa and telling him off, even Dad. Becca stood with a triumphant smirk on her round face. 'Tell-tale,' he hissed at her.

Alan slid into the room and Tim hated to think how wet he must seem. 'If you'd had an accident we'd never have known where you were,' Dad went on.

'I wasn't in the ruins,' he muttered. 'Just round the cliff.'

Mrs. Macpherson joined in then. 'Those paths aren't safe,' she said. 'And the cliffs at the end of the promontory are dangerous to climb. That's where ...'

Alan interrupted in a loud voice. 'Tara's hungry— where's the dog meat, Mum?'

His mother told him not to shout her down but she fed the dog and Tim fed Lucy. Mum said he must be punished and he should stay at home tomorrow when they went out—in his room. Becca grinned and went to bed. Tim wanted to run after her and hit her but Mum nagged him into having a bath and by the time he got to Becca's door, it was locked.

'I'll never speak to you again,' he hissed but she had her transistor on loudly.

Mum came to say goodnight. 'Sorry you'll be missing our trip tomorrow,' she said.

Dad came in then. 'I know what it's like, wanting to explore.' He smiled. 'But we worried about you.' He gave Tim a hug.

When they had gone, Tim got up, wrote on a large piece of drawing paper "I hate you: I'll never speak to you again all my life" and pushed it under Becca's door. On the way back down the creaking corridor, he met Alan. He wondered whether to tell him about the glowing eyes.

'I'd not like *her* for a sister,' Alan said.

A moment ago, Tim had wanted to kill Becca, now he was cross with Alan for pitying him.

'You could have fallen,' Alan said. 'Silly to go out like that. After all, you're a town boy and not used to scrambling on cliffs.'

Tim felt even crosser. 'At least my legs are OK,' he said. Then he felt guilty as Alan pushed past him without a word and slammed into his room.

Tim got into bed feeling all churned up and muddled. He was sad and angry. He shouldn't have said that to Alan. Lucy tried licking his ear to comfort him. Everything had gone wrong. He hadn't found the dirk; he had made an enemy of Alan and now he was supposed to stay in his room all the next morning. And Tim felt guilty too because he knew he wanted to be a hero—finding the treasure—even more than he wanted to help the Macphersons. Why should he care about this stupid Scottish family? Let Alan live in the town, as he was so scornful about town boys.

Well, he might just get into the other side of the house tomorrow and look at that book. It was something to do and it might give him another idea about the treasure. He *did* want to show them all he wasn't so puny and weedy.

He dreamed of gleaming green eyes, like Alan's but huge as saucers, advancing on him out of the darkness. He tried to run but his legs were glued to the ground. He tried to scream but nothing happened. The animal's hot breath was on his face and it was licking him.

When he woke Lucy was tenderly licking his face. Something howled outside and he took Lucy right into bed with him. She smelled of heather and earth and dog and he went to sleep.

CHAPTER SEVEN

When he woke up, Tim remembered his punishment and thought he wouldn't even go down to breakfast but hunger drove him to the kitchen and Lucy wanted to go out. Becca came in glaring at him and kicked his chair as she went past. His parents were looking at a map and did not notice.

Alan hobbled in, looking upset. 'Our best layer's gone. There's blood and some feathers (Tim shuddered) and a place where the creature's pushed through the bottom of the wire.'

'Didn't you count the hens when you shut them up?' Mrs. Macpherson asked.

'I thought they were all in. She must have been hiding in that nettlebed at the end of the run. That vermin! I'll get it!'

'A fox?' Dad asked.

'Wild-cat,' Alan said. 'I found hairs from its tail caught in the wire.'

'But you were angry with the gamekeeper for shooting at it,' Tim said. 'Now you want to kill it yourself.'

'It's different,' Alan mumbled.

'If Mr. Campbell wounded the cat then it would be better to shoot it,' said Mrs. Macpherson. 'Maybe that's why it's taken a hen—because it can't catch wild things any more.'

And because it has kittens, Tim thought.

'Do you think it might come back for another one?' Dad asked eagerly. 'I could wait up there with my camera, disguised as a bush.'

Mrs. Macpherson smiled at his enthusiasm and Tim felt embarrassed. Dad was just like a schoolboy sometimes. 'Well, I think we ought to block up the hole and make sure the hens are in. You would probably have more luck, Mr. Carter, down by the burn one night—if that's where it was before.'

Alan's slanting green eyes were narrowed with anger and his whole skinny body was tense, as if he might spring. Tim thought of those stories when men turned into wolves. Did Alan become a cat, springing on warm soft creatures, tearing . . .?

'Aren't you hungry, Tim?' Mum asked.

He looked down and saw the muddy brown sugar crusting his abandoned porridge.

'Time to get ready, Alan,' Mrs. Macpherson said. He went off, looking even more fierce. 'He hates his hospital visits. Of course he's had so many after the accident,' she said.

'Where did he fall—I mean, where on the coast?' Tim asked.

She was breaking an egg into the frying pan, and did not look up. 'From what we call the Black Rocks, at the end of Archnacross Head.'

For a moment the only sound was the egg spluttering in the frying-pan. Tim thought of that black cliff and the cave. Was Alan trying to find something? Did his father fall going after him?

'Well,' Dad looked round, trying to cover an awkward moment. 'I had a call from Wayland Scott this morning. He's asked me to go fishing in his boat while the others go to the sea. Sam wants to go with Becca.'

'I didn't realise Mrs. Macpherson would be out too—I wonder if you ought to stay here on your own, Tim,' Mum said.

'It's against the law to leave little children on their own,' Becca said nastily.

'I'm not a little child!' Tim shouted.

'Tara will keep out intruders,' Mrs. Macpherson said, 'and we'll be back in a couple of hours.'

Tim was left with a pile of sandwiches and Mum said they would be back in the early afternoon. Dad gave him a wink, meaning he was on his side but Becca went off without another word.

Tim waited until the Macphersons had gone to the hospital. The old house was so quiet that he could hear the grandfather clock ticking in the hall.

Lucy trotted after him as he fetched the key and opened the locked door. He was afraid that Alan, in his new, unfriendly mood, might have hidden the book away, but it was there, together with two more coke cans and half a packet of bacon-flavoured crisps. He found the new page Alan had been reading, with a crisp wedged in it for a bookmark.

'. . . Catherine Macpherson's body was found by the Loch. It was lying on the spot where tourists now come to see the Black Burn, as it is known locally, gush out from its rocky tunnel into the Loch. She had been shot. Perhaps she had been defending her son—it will never be known. Her younger son, Ian, survived this terrible day . . .'

So this was why Alan had gone to dig near the Loch.

Suddenly, through the open window, he heard a loud gunshot. Tara barked from the kitchen. He ran downstairs to the back door with the dogs at his heels. A second shot echoed through the ravine below and as he looked across he saw the promontory and the castle ruins. They were not ruins now: there was a tall, black castle with flames and smoke coming out of its narrow windows.

Fear filled him and he knew he must run over the heather, towards the ravine. Was the shot now or then? He ran and behind him he could hear the soldiers shout. They were hunting him down. Was he still Tim or was he the Alan of the past? Without knowing why, he ran to the place where the burn churned whitely into the dark tunnel of rock, the place where Catherine Macpherson of long ago had been shot.

Tara bounded ahead with Lucy. Then they both stopped and sniffed something on the ground.

Tim had to hide from those shadowy figures who were running after him. He looked into the bushes and saw a man, standing in the freckled shade holding a gun.

CHAPTER EIGHT

'Got her,' said Mr. Campbell.

Tim saw that the dogs were sniffing at a dead wild-cat. Its mouth was open in a death-snarl and the red blood oozed from the bullet-hole in its head. There was dried blood, too, on one paw. It was a lovely animal, beautifully striped with a flat head and bushy tail—almost as far removed from ginger Sandy at home as a tiger.

'She's full of milk,' the man said, picking up the body and slinging it into the churning water as if the cat were no more than old junk.

Tim thought of the kittens, somewhere, waiting for their mother, growing thin and then dying.

'I saw the cat, coming from the direction of the causeway,' Mr. Campbell went on. 'I suppose she might have come from the island when the causeway was dry.'

'The cave,' Tim blurted out without thinking. Then, as he saw Mr. Campbell looking at him, he realised that he had been thinking aloud and ran off with the dogs, as fast as he could, to the causeway.

Mr. Campbell was shouting at him as he ran. Tim looked back and saw the gillie pounding after him! The campers' tent was just ahead but they weren't outside.

The causeway was dry in the middle but the water was just beginning to lap over the sides. When he reached the island he looked back. Mr. Campbell was waving one arm in angry jerks from the end of the causeway and he was carrying his gun.

Tim thought of the kittens—the gillie would shoot them or just throw them into the sea. He had to save them.

He ran along the narrow path, sweat dripping off him because it had suddenly grown very hot with a yellow-grey sky above. He wished he hadn't worn his anorak. The dogs followed him as he slithered down into the little cove.

At first he thought it was a seagull crying. But the mewing came from the cave where he had seen the eyes. His track shoes were wet so he took them off and began to climb up the rock, clinging to ledges with his toes. The dogs whined below him.

At home, Becca climbed the trees in the park and he had to struggle to get to the first branch because he was so much shorter and his arms weren't strong. But the kittens' cries made him hurry. It was a difficult climb, and he looked back once and nearly fell. Mr. Campbell was shouting from the cliff path and Tara was growling, in her deep voice, forgetting her usual gentle wolfhound ways. Lucy barked a challenge. Would the man follow? At least he couldn't bring the gun too.

There were white chicken feathers and a hen's head on the ledge. This made him feel sick and he almost gave up then. Why was he trying to rescue animals who could kill so savagely? Then he remembered the dreadful sight of the Christmas turkey in the larder, when he was four. People ate birds so why couldn't the wildcats? The plaintive mewing increased and he had to haul himself up with the remainder of his strength.

His knee hurt where the rock had rubbed through the jeans but he was there. He crawled into a dark cave, which was just big enough for a boy, and put his hand forward. The mewing changed to hissing and spitting and needle-sharp teeth bit into his fingers.

Now his eyes were used to the dark he saw two little shapes just ahead.

'Hey—I'll get those kits. Leave them to me!' shouted Mr. Campbell from outside. The growling increased. 'Get off, ye great beastie . . .' Scottish-sounding swear words abounded.

Tim scrabbled among feathers and something soft and nasty-feeling, to catch the kittens. He was bitten again as he picked them up. One, two—warm and hissing. He put one in each anorak pocket and thrust his hands deep into the back of the cave to make sure there weren't any more. His fingers felt something hard and rounded, then he moved to the right and grasped a heavy bit of metal. He crawled to the opening of the cave, holding his weapon ready to defend the kittens.

'You can't have them!' he shouted down. Mr. Campbell was below, trying to climb. Tara was pulling at his trousers and Lucy darted at his feet. Suddenly the man kicked out and hurt Lucy, who cringed away, whining, with tail down. Tim was hot with fury. Nobody hit Lucy and got away with it!

Tim waved the heavy metal thing. 'Get off!' he yelled and then he heard himself shouting out in a strange language. Or was it the boy who was crouched beside him in the opening of the cave? He could feel the boy's bony shoulders pressing against his in the narrow opening and he turned a moment to see a pale freckled face, streaked with dust and sweat and green cat's eyes looking through a tangle of wild red hair. He even felt the boy's panting breath on him and smelled his fear.

Tim felt no fear this time and when the boy put out his hand gave him the lump of metal. It was only then that he saw it was a short, rusty sword with a carved handle, eroded by time.

The dirk flashed in the air. The boy cried out in that wild language and Mr. Campbell, who had nearly reached the opening, swore as he fell. He lay still on the flat rock. The dogs growled at him then Lucy forgave him and began licking his face.

The boy had gone but the dirk lay on the little ledge among the chicken feathers. Tim thrust it into his jeans' pocket and started to climb down the rock.

The kittens were mewing now and he worried that they would climb out of his pockets, or were they too small? Thinking about them took his mind off the difficult climb down. There was a shout from the water as he slithered and slid and nearly fell. He clung desperately and somehow found a foothold, then he slid down the last few feet and landed on top of Tara, who was guarding Mr. Campbell.

'Tim!' shouted his father. There was *Wildcat* a short way from the promontory and his father and Mr. Scott were waving at him. Supposing Mr. Campbell was dead? He did not dare look but put his track shoes on again, pulled Tara away and somehow got himself and the dogs up the steep path. His arms and legs felt shaky and weak after all the shocks and he heard the chug of the *Wildcat*'s engine coming right up to the headland.

'Come back!' called his father, as Tim lay panting on the path. He looked down. They were coming into the cove in a small dinghy which they had paddled from the anchored *Wildcat*. Soon they would find the gillie. He tried to face the fact that he might have killed a man. It was like the worst kind of nightmare and he wished he could wake up in his own bed at home. Tara was obediently trotting along the track with Lucy beside her, heading for the causeway.

Tim felt in his pockets to see if the kittens were all right and needle-sharp teeth dug into his fingers. The yellowish-black clouds hid the sun completely now and it was oppressively hot when he reached the causeway.

It was covered with water. He carried Lucy and did not stop to take off his track shoes, somehow comforted by the sight of Tara half-swimming, half-walking through the water ahead. The rubber of his soles slipped on the rock and twice he almost fell. Then the air thickened and the thunder rolled round the Loch as if it had been tossed from mountain to mountain.

Becca laughed at him during storms, when he drew the curtains and lay with his head under a cushion.

'No, no!' he sobbed as sheet lightning flashed across the water.

The storm was like his worst nightmare. His legs were so tired he could hardly drag them along and every time the lightning flashed he thought it would strike him. He'd be punished for killing Mr. Campbell. Becca had told him that lightning struck right through you and left you shrivelled and black 'and then you crumble into a pile of black powder' she had added. He sobbed as he ran, imagining himself a pile of black powder. In this rain it would be turned to mud and then people would step on him. 'Brush that nasty mud off your shoes, Becca,' he imagined Mum saying and there he would be, spread all over the doormat.

Somehow he got across the water and then the rain came down, at first big drops, then soon a solid wall, so it beat on his face and clogged up his eyelids. For a moment he thought he'd stop and wriggle into the empty tent but the kittens needed proper shelter. Already his thin anorak was soaked through. He took out the damp, faintly spitting kittens and put them into the front of his tee-shirt, tucking it into his belt so they would not fall out. He felt their damp warmth and worried about them as he ran on but the kittens made the storm seem less scaring.

There was the house as last! Alan and his mother might be back by now. Mrs. Macpherson might very well object to the kittens, especially as the wildcat had killed her hen. He'd have to hide them in Alan's secret room. If he went down the coal-shute nobody would see him.

Lucy whined as he fiddled with the coal flap. Tara nosed at his legs. 'Home,' he ordered her, waving his arm and she ran off towards the house door. Lucy was soaked, so he pushed her down the coal shute first and then slid in, braking with his feet and holding the kittens against him with one hand. The noise of the storm raged above as he groped through the cellar and found the stairs. He struggled up, so tired that he could not think any more and he nearly fell down the hole in the landing.

At last he reached Alan's room and carefully took the kittens out of his pocket. Despite his shirt, they were wet and cold. They must be dried or they would die. He looked round but only saw the banner on the wall, so he tore it down and gently rubbed the kittens' fur. Lucy, soaked and shivering, stood on her hind legs as he wrapped the little creatures in the aged, cracking material and put them in a sagging chair under the window. She whined and made a little pleased sound in her throat. Then she was up, giving them a lick before he could stop her. The kittens hissed a little and she turned each one over, thoroughly washing their small stomachs.

He sat back on his heels, feeling light-headed with tiredness and the dreadful sight of the gillie lying in the cove, imprinted on his brain. He tried to think only of the kittens. The sky outside was getting light as the storm died down and he saw the kittens' blue eyes were open, so they must be at least two weeks old. But how could he feed them? Maybe they would drink out of a doll's feeding bottle but that meant telling Alan and going to the shops. He wanted these kittens to be his secret. He might have to tell Alan, though, if the Police took him away . . .

The little dog curled happily round her babies. Tim was wondering what to do next when Alan came into the room with Tara.

'Where did you find them?' he asked, putting his hand out to the kittens. Gentle Lucy growled protectively. 'I found Tara outside, barking, and you weren't in your room—I guessed you were here.'

Tim's words were all jumbled like his thoughts. 'That gamekeeper—killed the mother, so I rescued the kittens . . . and is this the dirk?'

He gave it to Alan, who rubbed at the shaft and two dull red jewels began to shine through the sand and dirt, just like those on the dirk in the picture above them.

'Tell me about it later,' Alan said. 'Let's get back first so Mum doesn't see the key's gone and find us here. She's got those campers in the kitchen. We picked them up on the way back from the hospital, in the storm.'

'The kittens,' Tim said. 'I won't let you kill them!' He felt like a mother wildcat himself, wild and fierce.

'I don't want to kill them,' Alan said. 'Leave your dog with them and we'll come back with the milk. Give me the key.'

Where was the key? Part of Tim's mind was numb: frozen with shock and fear. Then he saw it, next to the old book. Alan had just locked the door when they heard a car drawing up.

'It's Mr. Scott, or maybe the Police!' Tim said in a shaky voice. 'Mr. Campbell might be dead!'

CHAPTER NINE

'You're all streaked with coal,' Mum kept on saying.

'I bet you were scared in the storm, Timmo,' said Becca.

'You promised not to go out,' said Mum.

'You might have got killed on that cliff!' said Mr. Scott.

'Is he dead?' Tim asked and felt sick.

They were all in the kitchen and everyone was talking at once. They had returned in two cars, Dad and Mr. Scott in the Rolls and Mum, Becca and Sam in their old car, driven away from the beach by the storm. The two campers were looking puzzled and damp by the stove.

'Is who dead?' asked Mrs. Macpherson.

'Mr. Campbell—he fell from the black rocks and it was my fault.'

Alan went very white but he moved away when Mr. Scott tried to pat his shoulder.

'He's all right,' said Dad, hugging Tim, whose knees went weak with relief.

Mr. Scott smiled reassuringly. 'You're Daddy and I,

Tim, managed to find the doctor's office open and he said it was just a bang on the head and a few bruises. He's to take it real easy for a couple of days and have an X-ray to make certain sure. And his wife is fussing round him right now. He seems to think that Tim here went for him with a dirk, he called it. I think that's just what that bump did to him. He's a surly fellow at the best of times.'

'A knife? But you haven't got one,' Mum said.

'What was he chasing you for, Tim?' Sam asked.

Alan nudged him. 'He'd killed a wildcat and thought Tim knew where her kittens were.'

'Kittens—did you find dear little kittens?' Sam asked, looking excited.

'They were dead,' Alan said.

But how were they going to keep the kittens secret? Tim was so relieved that the gillie wasn't dead that he hardly cared. He could see that Alan wouldn't want Sam poking about in his secret room.

'Oh, what a pity!' Dad said. 'I read somewhere of a man who reared a wildcat and it became quite tame.'

'That's right,' said the bearded camper, rubbing his hair with a towel.

'I guess I shall have to tell Campbell not to shoot wildcats,' Mr. Scott said. 'I'm real sad about those little kittens. We need to preserve the native species in this wonderful country of yours.'

Alan glowered at him. Tim thought the American gushed a lot but maybe he meant it, like Dad always going on about 'dramatic' views and all that.

'And why, Tim, did you go out when you were supposed to be staying in your room?' Mum asked. 'And that's another pair of jeans you've ruined. I'll need to patch them.'

'I heard a shot,' he said. 'I wanted to know what was happening.'

'Any excuse! I thought I could trust you. And you might have got badly hurt.'

'Sorry,' said Tim. He could stand up to her when she was cross but not when she sounded disappointed.

'And why are you covered with coal?'

'I'll go and wash it off,' he said quickly.

Mrs. Macpherson and the woman camper, who was called Poppy, were making tea and putting anoraks to dry. The storm had changed to a light pattering rain.

Mr. Scott was talking about the fishing trip. 'I knew he'd just love to fish,' he said. 'We caught a real big one before we spotted young Tim on the rock. Ben here thinks it's a bass.'

The fish was brought out of the Rolls and Mr. Scott gave it to Mrs. Macpherson with a little bow. 'For you, my dear,' he said as if it was a bunch of roses. 'And because we have had the pleasure of visiting with you here.'

'Sucking up,' he heard Alan murmur in his ear.

'Mum took us to the beach and there were heaps of holidaymakers and we were swimming—it was cold as ice and then the storm started and I wanted to go on swimming . . .' Becca rambled on.

'And was I glad of that storm!' said Sam. 'This Scots sea is real cold.'

Tim saw Alan creeping out of the kitchen with a mug in his hand and he slipped out after him saying, 'Just going to wash.'

'Someone might see,' Tim said as Alan opened the door again.

'They'll be busy for a while,' he said. 'Those kittens must be fed. I kept the key in my pocket, after all.'

One kitten was curled up, asleep but the other was kneading away at Lucy's teat and trying to suck.

'They only have milk when they have pups, don't they?' Tim asked. Lucy was stretched out, her black rubbery lips parted in a happy smile, showing her small white teeth. 'Her pups were sold six months ago.'

'I suppose she's just being motherly,' Alan said. 'We can

try giving them milk on our fingers. I should think they're about two or three weeks old so there's a chance of rearing them.'

The smaller kitten, woken up, just sneezed at the drop of milk and turn away fretfully miaowing. Its fluffy fur was drying but it looked weak and tired. Lucy muttered but did not bite as Alan disentangled the bigger kit from her and tried the milk on his finger. It hissed at him and then licked a little off but Lucy fussed, cleaning its face, and soon it was back to her teat, sucking away. 'No milk for you there, little one,' said Alan.

Tim remembered something. 'One of Lucy's pups was a weakling. Mum used to feed it with a medicine dropper until it died.'

Alan grunted. 'That's it. I've seen one of those in our bathroom cupboard. I'll fetch it later. We'd better go now.'

They left the dirk behind with Lucy and the kittens. 'It seems right there,' Alan said, looking happy. 'Now we have the dirk, we're bound to find the treasure soon, then we won't have to sell. I shall build up the castle and live in it when I grow up.'

They hurried downstairs and waited behind the door. They heard footsteps in the hall and held their breath. Supposing Mrs. Macpherson had found that the key had gone? But the footsteps went on, towards the stairs.

'Mum's gone upstairs to look for you,' Becca said when they came into the kitchen. 'You're still dirty. Where did you go?'

Tim washed his face at the sink. He glanced at Alan, who was hovering near the key peg, ready to put it back as soon as his mother's back was turned. Sam and Becca were giggling together and watching Alan. 'They both look guilty,' Tim heard Becca whisper.

Mum came in. 'I went to get you,' she said to Tim. 'You do keep on disappearing and your face has a tide-mark all round.'

'The only way to stop him going off is to keep him with us,' Dad said. 'After all, we've only another three days here so he must see something of the area. He can clean the car as a punishment when he gets home.'

He was being kind, as usual. He didn't realise that what Tim wanted was to be sent to his room all the time now, so he could slip out and hunt for treasure and also feed the kittens. Only three days left! The legend of the dirk had better be true and bring them luck quite soon. He didn't want to leave Archnacross House, he realised. Finding the kittens had made him friends with Alan. Quarrelling with Becca in the little London house seemed very boring, even with the museums, park and swimming-pool.

The campers had changed now and were hanging out their wet jeans round the range. 'We're staying the night,' Poppy announced happily. 'Mrs. Macpherson has been very kind to us and offered us a room.'

Tim thought that would be one more lot of people to avoid if he had to creep out in the night.

'How did the hospital visit go?' Mum asked Mrs. Macpherson, who was pouring out third cups of tea and adding home-made pancakes to the picnic sandwiches, damp from the beach. Tim found he was starving, after all the fear and tension.

'They say he's doing fine,' she began but she was interrupted by Alan. 'The kettle's boiling over!'

It wasn't but he put the key back and hobbled out of the room.

'Alan's often in pain, isn't he? I've seen his face,' said Mr. Scott.

'Yes, he is,' said his mother. 'Quite often but he won't admit it. Well, the truth is he'll not get much better than he is, they say, even with the exercises and treatment.'

'I'm sure if I got him back to the States I could find just the right doctor for him,' said Mr. Scott.

71

'He's seen a fine specialist here,' said Mrs. Macpherson. 'But thank you for the idea.'

'He doesn't like you, that's why he won't come out in the boat,' said Becca.

'Becca!' said Mum.

'Yeah, I guess it's because he doesn't want to lose his home,' Sam said thoughtfully. 'I bet I'd feel the same, too.'

'And I have the surveyor and planning people coming round tomorrow,' Mr. Scott said sadly.

'So you *are* selling?' Dad asked Mrs. Macpherson.

'I've agreed, yes,' she said. She went to the sink and began to clean and fillet the fish, her bony shoulders hunched as if she didn't want them to see her face.

Tim slid out of the room to tell Alan. They must do something right now, even if it meant getting into more trouble. He found Alan in his bedroom, staring gloomily out of the window at the rain. Far off, thunder rumbled in distant hills. Alan's room was at the back like Tim's. It was filled with interesting-looking things: gulls' eggs, bird skeletons, stones and pebbles with bits of quartz. Tim noticed football boots and a cricket bat in a corner and almost wished he and Alan could change places. There he was, able to play games and no good at them and Alan loving games and not able to play.

'The Loch really does look black,' Tim said, staring out.

'We've got to get back to the cave,' said Alan. 'The treasure must be there. Did you feel anything, a bundle or something hard?'

Tim remembered the round hard thing . . . 'Sort of,' he said. 'But if she died by the burn, how could she have taken the treasure to the cave?'

'She went with him, to save him from the soldiers, then when he was killed, ran back to the burn . . . the book could have got it wrong. After all, it's over 200 years ago,' Alan said. 'She might have been on her way back to her younger son.'

'I saw . . .' Tim began. It was still difficult to speak of the ghosts. 'The boy, he was there beside me in the cave, on his own. And I've seen her running over the heather and also in the kitchen-garden. Maybe she tried to draw the soldiers off Alan.'

'Like a mother bird does,' Alan said.

The ghosts flitted about in Tim's memory. You could call them a 'confusion of ghosts' he thought.

'Maybe he was wounded at the burn,' Alan said.

Tim thought hard. 'Perhaps there's no time in their place. Time is different—like in outer space. So I just see a sort of muddle of happenings.' He remembered something he had been wanting to ask. 'Were you trying to get to that cave in the Black Rocks when you and your Dad had the accident?'

'Yes,' Alan answered. 'He was interested in wildcats and we'd seen one in the castle ruins and then followed it to that cove. It was January and the rocks were icy. I should have known better. I climbed up, you see, though Dad told me not to, then my foot slipped just below the cave and Dad climbed nearer to help. It started to sleet and then the wildcat must have heard us. It hissed and sprang out onto that little ledge, making me jump. I slipped sideways. Dad tried to put his hand out to save me and we both fell. He hit his head on the rocky cove floor.' He turned his head away but Tim knew he was crying. 'It was my fault, you know.'

Tim didn't know what to do. He put out his hand and patted Alan's shoulder as Mum did when he was upset but Alan jerked away. 'It wasn't your fault,' Tim said.

'I think it was,' said Alan. 'Dad didn't die right away. I heard him saying, "the boy . . . saw the boy fighting. They got him." I hadn't found the book then so I didn't know what boy he was talking about. Mum hinted sometimes that Dad saw things. Do you think he saw the "ghost Alan"?'

Tim knew he could help. 'Yes,' he said firmly, having no idea if it was true or not. 'And I think that made him fall.'

Alan grabbed his arm. 'You think so? You really do? All the time I was crawling up the cliff to get help and it took a long while because my leg hurt so much—all that time I wanted to die because I'd killed him.'

'You crawled up there, with your leg and foot broken?' Tim tried to imagine it. He'd broken a finger once, playing cricket and he remembered the pain and how it made him hate cricket ever after. Alan must be as brave as he had always wanted to be. Alan looked as if he wished he'd not said so much. He ran off to get the medicine dropper from the bathroom.

There was no chance after that to visit the kittens because they had to finish the sandwiches and then play Scrabble and Racing Demon. The campers were very jolly and hearty and kept asking for another game. Sam won each time, just beating Tim which made him cross. He was used to winning at home. When they stopped for tea, Mum looked round. 'Where's Lucy?' she asked.

'Upstairs,' Tim said, which was true. He wondered nervously if she would bark and if she did, whether the others would hear and find out about the secret room.

The Scotts got up to go home at last and Mrs. Macpherson asked them to come back for supper when they had called on Mr. Campbell, to see how he was. They accepted gladly. Mrs. Macpherson seemed actually to *like* Mr. Scott. Or was she being nice to him so he didn't change his mind about buying the house? Tim looked at Alan. How could they get away?

Dad suggested a stroll down to the Loch, as it had stopped raining but Mum said she must mend and wash Tim's jeans or he'd have nothing to wear. 'I'll fetch them,' he said, to stop her going upstairs and finding Lucy wasn't there.

'Bring Lucy down. She must need to go out,' Mum said.

Now, what could he do? Should he go back and say she wouldn't move? Lucy couldn't stay in Alan's secret room, anyway. She needed her dinner and she always slept on Tim's bed at night. For a moment, it all seemed so difficult that he wondered whether it would be easier to tell the grown-ups about the kittens. Dad would be very excited but if Mrs. Macpherson was going to live in the town, she wouldn't be able to keep them.

Alan was hovering near the key peg again and he gave Tim a warning look as he went out of the room.

Tim had an idea but it meant telling a lie, which he didn't enjoy. He ran up and down stairs, fetching the jeans and calling Lucy as he ran down. He was just going to say he couldn't find her and that she must have wandered outside, when Tara barked and Mrs. Macpherson opened the door to the campers, who had been to fetch their dried-off sleeping-bags.

Alan winked at Tim, took the key and they both slid out and up into the other side of the house.

The bigger kitten was sucking at Lucy but the smaller one lay curled up, near the hilt of the dirk. It did not move.

Alan felt it. 'Dead,' he said. 'Perhaps it was a weakling. Or it caught cold.' They stood silently, feeling sad. Lucy gave the dead kitten a lick, then went back to the live one, as if she knew there was no point in wasting her time. Alan put the dead kitten in an old cardboard box. 'I'll bury it in the Animals' Graveyard,' he said.

'Do you mean that one near the hen run? I thought it was for *people*,' Tim said.

Alan laughed. 'No, our family are buried in the churchyard, just down the road. But the pets' graveyard is very old—we've always buried our animals there.' He tried the remaining kitten with the milk from the medicine dropper. At first it struggled and hissed a bit, then swallowed a few drops.

Tim decided he ought to take Lucy back before Mum asked about her. She whined and struggled. She had found one of her lost puppies and didn't want to give it up.

'You'll have to bring her back for the night,' Alan said. 'Otherwise the kitten might die.'

In the kitchen, everyone was talking and hardly noticed when Tara sniffed at Lucy, almost as if the dogs were talking too, about the kittens. Tim and Alan went to shut up the hens. They splashed through great puddles; the bolting lettuces had been flattened to the ground and the bushes beside the narrow path were bowed with rain. The setting sun, struggling down in a shaft through the clouds, lit the windows of the house again, so it looked as if on fire.

'After supper we'll go back to the cave,' Alan said as he drove the last hen inside its house.

'Mum will kill me if I go there again,' Tim said. 'And I bet Becca and Sam will be nosing after us.'

'We'll just make a dash for it and when we come back with the treasure, they'll be so pleased they won't mind. Remember, we'll find it now we have the dirk so it won't matter what happens then.'

Mr. Scott and Sam arrived with a whole salmon, cooked by Mr. Scott's housekeeper, and a great dish of home-made strawberry ice-cream, bottles of wine and cans of coke.

'Just a little to help you out,' he said, smiling.

'He's just a show-off,' Alan said later when he and Tim had escaped, saying they must give the dogs a run. It had been easier than they thought, as the wine had made the grown-ups flushed and merry and Sam and Becca were both eating seconds of strawberry ice-cream.

'Throwing his money about like that,' Alan went on as they jogged over the heather. 'Well, we'll soon be richer than he is.'

Tim didn't say anything but he did have a moment's doubt. Supposing the treasure, when they found it, wasn't worth such a lot after all? The way Alan went on now, you'd think they were going to discover gold bars and diamonds.

Tim kept hoping to see the ghosts but the wet heather was empty and the Loch shore was crowded with gulls, eating bits brought up by the storm. They ran across the causeway, where the waters had receded, and left the dogs at the top of the cliff path. Lucy fussed but settled down by Tara at last. She whined restlessly, obviously longing to get back to the kitten.

Tim did not want to go back to the cave. His legs still ached from the last climb and he felt something dreadful might happen. Supposing it wasn't true, that the dirk brought good luck? Supposing the ghosts came back and made Alan fall and get killed? Then he thought that was silly—Alan's ancestor wouldn't want him killed, or his father for that matter—ghosts just appeared. Perhaps they weren't able to be helpful or angry but just had to go on acting the same part.

He shivered all the same. The sun, setting in a mass of dark purple clouds, threw a dark shadow from the cliff across the little cove. Great puddles of rain and Loch water made the smooth black rock slippery. 'I don't like it here,' Alan said as if he knew what Tim was thinking. 'I keep remembering.'

They took off their wet track shoes and started to climb but Alan cried out. His face was white. 'It's my leg,' he said. 'I canna do it.' He sounded angry. 'Take my torch,' he ordered.

So Tim went on alone and Alan sat on the rocky floor of the cove. Tim grew more scared as he climbed. He was so tired and the rock was very wet from the storm. His foot slipped and dangled in the air.

'To the left, there's a crack,' Alan called up.

Tim hung on with every muscle of his thin arms, straining and scrabbling wildly, fingers slipping. At any moment he would fall . . . fall . . .

His bare toes gripped a ledge.

At last he was pulling himself onto the ledge and into the cave. He shone the torch round. There was the bundle of cloth, partly torn by the cat to make a nest. He picked it up and saw it was a piece of ancient tartan material, crisp and tattered with age.

He shone the torch further, to the back of the cave, which sloped down only a few feet from the front. Something white lay half-buried in the sand. He scrabbled at it and then saw what it was.

A human skull grinned at him!

CHAPTER TEN

'A skull,' Alan said in a shaky voice.

'It's smallish—it must be his, that other Alan's',' Tim whispered. 'It's not big enough to be a grown-up's.' Somehow he couldn't breathe. He had nearly fallen again, rushing out of the cave and down the rock.

'Did you look underneath it to see if the treasure was there?' Alan asked.

'No,' said Tim. 'I bet you wouldn't either.'

Then he tried, sitting on the cove floor, to think what might have happened. 'She wouldn't have put the treasure under her son's body. I mean if they killed Alan there and then saw her go into the cave with the treasure, the soldiers would have followed and taken it. Or if Alan had it, then they were certain to have seen the bundle.'

'Time to get back before the grown-ups find we've gone so far,' Alan said.

When they got to the top of the cliff the dogs greeted them, then looked down the path and barked.

'Someone's coming,' Alan said.

Sam and Becca stood on the path, grinning. 'We've caught you out,' Becca shouted. 'Going back to this place where you fell. Tell us what you're looking for and then I won't say I saw you here again, Tim.'

'I can't tell you,' he said. 'And anyway you shouldn't be here either.' He and Alan ran on and over the causeway with the girls following.

'You look pretty white and scared, almost as if you'd seen a ghost,' Becca said. 'We were right above you in the castle ruins. And we saw you climbing down the cliff, Timmo. Did you know the gang at school call him Timmo the Timid because he's scared of everything?' she said to Sam.

Tim charged at her, took her by surprise and left her lying winded on the heather. Sam charged back but Alan did a kind of rugger tackle and brought her down just as Mum, Dad and Mr. Scott came hurrying towards them.

'And what are you doing, fighting girls?' Mum asked.

'I'm smaller than Becca,' Tim said.

'And I guess Sam can take care of herself,' said Mr. Scott, just as Sam stood up and threw Alan over her shoulder with the greatest ease.

'Judo,' said her father.

Sam ran to Alan. 'Are you OK?' Is your leg all right?'

'Get away with you, woman,' Alan shouted.

Tim was taken into the kitchen for yet another boring lecture. Becca and Sam admitted they had been to the ruins so Tim and Becca were sent to bed early and Sam winked at Tim as she went home with her father.

Darkness was falling and Mrs. Macpherson turned on the lights but the electricity wasn't working. 'The power cable must have come down in that storm,' she said. She lit candles and gave the children one each, stuck into old mugs. 'Be very careful to put them out,' she warned. Mum blew Tim's candle out when she came to say goodnight.

'You have your torch if you need the bathroom,' she said. 'Don't light the candle. It's always a risk.'

Lucy was whining by his door, thinking of her new puppy. Tim was very tired but he had to keep awake until everyone came to bed. Then he and Alan could take Lucy to the kitten. He put his head under the bedclothes clutching her comforting warmth, thinking of the skull and the little dog licked his chin. He heard the old corridor creak as the grown-ups came to bed. His eyelids grew very heavy.

He was woken by Alan shaking him. 'They've all gone to sleep,' he said. 'Better bring Lucy up to the kitten now.'

The little creature was calling plaintively as they came in. Lucy hurled herself at it, licked it all over and then spread herself flat so it could suck her teats.

Alan tried the medicine-dropper again. The kitten opened its mouth reluctantly and took some milk. Then it struggled to get back to Lucy. 'I hope it'll be OK. It didn't take much,' Alan said. 'I think we ought to stay here and keep trying to feed it otherwise it could be dead by morning.'

Moonlight filtered into the room but it was rather dark so he put the candle on an old box by the chair. 'We can look at the book again. I think she might have hidden the treasure in the cellar, in a secret room where the other son, Ian, might have been hiding. Mum said the cellars were the oldest part of the house and they'd have remained if most of it was burned. I did see some loose bricks in the cellar wall.' He sounded wide awake and excited while Tim was still yawning.

'I'll fetch a couple of blankets from my room. We can take it in turns to sleep,' Alan said. 'You'd better stay here in case Lucy barks. I'd better warm up some more milk, too.'

The rising wind banged the door behind him and made the candle flicker and send alarming shadows round the room.

Fear made Tim pick up the dirk and hold it. He rubbed at the blade, removing sand and dirt and saw there were words engraved on it. He took it right up to the window to look when a wildcat screeched loudly outside. Lucy stirred and growled protectively. The wind was blowing wild white clouds over the full moon and the cat called again from the direction of the hen run. Was it the wildcat's mate?

The silvered ranks of lettuces and cabbages disappeared and he saw yet again the dark writhing shapes of the apple trees, burning, and the woman running with the dark bundle under her arm.

The wildcat called again. Was that in the past or in the present? He knew, almost as if someone had told him, that he must follow the woman this time and on his own.

He went downstairs, creeping across the hall. He heard Alan in the kitchen, whispering to Tara as he heated the milk. Then he unbolted the front door and dashed out.

In the orchard the smoke made him cough and he could smell the sweetness of smouldering apple wood and see the flames eating the pale blossom. One of the soldiers ahead turned and ran towards him. Another man followed and he heard their breathing, sharp and rasping. One of them was coughing. He flung out the dirk in his hand and it pierced through a tattered sleeve as if it had been a shred of mist. The man ran on, as if nothing had happened. The soldiers must have lost sight of the woman, so they were doubling back to look for her. As Tim went forward, burning cinders fell on his face and arms but did not hurt him. Then he saw a dark shape, crouching, half-hidden by a big water-butt in the far corner of the orchard.

The shape moved and the woman ran round the butt and through the doorway in the wall. Tim followed, expecting at any moment she would disappear and he would be back in the present. But she ran on down the narrow path through a kind of tunnel made by low fruit trees grown together at the top. This led past the place where the hen run was now, through a dark arch cut in thick, strong-smelling yews. A half-moon shone above the animals' graveyard. The small headstones were newer-looking, some gleaming white, and the grass between the graves clipped neatly.

Catherine Macpherson ran to a grave and he saw the bunch of bluebells on the newly heaped earth and then, beyond, the boy stood up from his hiding place. The moonlight flashed on the dirk as the boy used it to dig the freshly turned earth.

Tim stood stupidly in the confusion of past and present, thinking it was the wrong time of year for bluebells. Then he saw the woman burying the bundle and covering it with earth. The boy tugged at her arm and they both ran out of the far corner of the graveyard.

Tim followed as they went through an iron gate in the wall beyond and then over the heather, towards the burn. He had gone only a few yards after them when he heard a hoarse shout and saw the two soldiers running from the direction of the house. 'Look out! They're after you again!' he shouted, running too. He heard a dog barking from the house, turned and saw a flicker of fire, not from the orchard this time but from that top window which was Alan's secret room.

This was the Past, he thought. But he looked again and the woman, boy and following soldiers had gone and the moor lay quiet under the full moon. The wildcat was howling and the dog barking. He ran back through the gap in the broken wall, past the hen-run and down the narrow path where wet grasses rasped his legs.

When he was in the kitchen-garden he saw the little flame had grown bigger and smoke came out of Alan's window!

CHAPTER ELEVEN

By the time he reached the house, the moonlight was whitening the thick black smoke that came through the window. Lucy had stopped barking. Was she struggling to breathe?

He ran for the front door, his heart pounding. Was Alan back in the room? How long had he been in the Past? The hall was empty and there was no sound from the rest of the house, except Tara, scratching and whining at the kitchen door as if she knew something was wrong. He let her through and called but Alan did not reply. Afterwards, he wondered why he hadn't shouted for help but his one thought then was that Lucy and the kitten and perhaps Alan, too, were in danger.

He opened the door leading to the staircase and fell back, choking, as smoke poured down. Should he wake the others? 'Fire!' he called but he was sure nobody would hear in the other part of the house. If he ran to find them, a little dog like Lucy would die quickly. Later, he felt guilty that his first thoughts had been for Lucy, not Alan. He shut the door. He'd have to go up from the cellar steps—it might be easier that way. As he ran past the kitchen sink he remembered something he had read, and wetted a drying-up cloth, tying it over his nose and chin.

Tara bounded behind him as he ran down to the cellar guided by the faint splodge of moonlight from the kitchen. At the bottom it was very dark but he found the other door and steps and went up, feeling his way on hands and knees.

As he reached the top, smoke billowed round him and he coughed. He remembered his imaginary rescues. He had read somewhere that the worst of the smoke was high up. Tara pushed past him, head low, and both of them just escaped falling into the open hole. He felt the wind on his head. The polythene cover on the roof hole must have blown off.

Tara gave a muffled bark and bounded into the room. Smoke choked his throat and smarted his eyes so he could only just see Alan, a dim shape on the floor, clutching the little bundles of fur that were Lucy and the kitten. Tara whined and licked him and Alan gave a faint choking cry.

The curtains blazed and the flames had spread to the old chair, which gave out a horrible smell of burning horsehair and dense smoke. Should he break a window for air? Then he remembered that a draught made fire flare up.

He picked up Lucy and the kitten and crawled out, so the increasing smoke rose above him. Were they dead? Sobbing now, he crawled round the hole in the landing and put them down, out of range of the worst smoke. How could he leave Alan? He struggled back into the room as the flaming curtains fell and new flames shot up from the old rug. He pulled at Alan's feet, impeded by Tara, as she growled and stood guard over the boy. The wet towel was slipping and drying in the hot air and he felt sweat running down his face as he pushed Tara back.

'Come on, come on!' he shouted at Alan in a smoke-choked voice. Why was such a thin boy so heavy? The smoke was making him feel dizzy and each breath was a rasping effort. He dragged at Alan's legs again and slapped at Tara. The great dog, unused to blows, cringed back and now there was someone beside him, a boy in a ragged plaid. The freckles stood out on his pale face against the dark smoke and Tim thought he was smiling as he crouched down and pulled at Alan's legs. With his help it was easy getting Alan through the door.

Suddenly, there was a slithering crash and a howl of pain from Tara.

Tim looked for the boy, but he had gone. He was alone and couldn't move. His arms and legs felt weighted down as he lay exhausted against Alan, feeling the ancient cold damp of the cellar floor icy against his boiling skin. There was a faint glow from the top of the stairs leading to the cellar and he heard the distant crackle of the fire. He realised he ought to have closed the door to stop it spreading.

His eyes were swollen and streaming and he wheezed as he breathed. He thought he had passed out because Lucy and the kitten were weights on his chest, lying limp. Dimly he remembered going back for them after he and the boy had pulled Alan down the stairs. Were they dead? He struggled to sit up and then he thought he heard a faint spitting from the kitten and Lucy coughed.

He felt weak with relief. What about Alan, though? He wasn't moving. Tim knew he couldn't get him up those other steps, to the kitchen. He tried to cry for help but his voice was so hoarse. Why hadn't the others woken up? The fire would spread to the rest of the house and they would be in terrible danger. He must move but he was so tired, as if life itself was leaking away, leaving him helpless.

Then Alan coughed and was horribly sick. 'Tara,' he croaked. She was trapped in the burning room . . . Tim began to cry.

There was a loud banging somewhere and shouting, then footsteps and more shouting. He called out, coughing and choking but somehow forcing a cry out of his smoke-filled lungs. There was an answering shout, then a square of light showed as someone opened the door and shone a big flashlight down.

Then they were all there, Mr. Scott first. Dimly, Tim wondered how he had got there. He was almost too tired to be thankful that they were alive. 'Tara's up in the old bit . . .' he manged to croak as they were carried into the kitchen.

'The big dog's in the fire?' Sam asked. Tim wondered what she was doing there. Mum came running, dragging along Becca in pyjamas. 'Couldn't get her to wake up,' she panted. Poppy and her husband were already filling buckets in the kitchen and they staggered into the hall with them.

'Sam—no!' shouted Mr. Scott just as Sam went through the door to the cellar and he rushed after her.

'They'll be killed!' shouted Mrs. Macpherson and tried to follow but Dad caught her arm. They had a kind of struggle—almost funny if Tim hadn't been so upset—Dad a weird chunky figure in his patched brown dressing-gown and Mrs. Macpherson taller than he, wearing a track suit.

'All outside,' Dad ordered calmly. He might be short and vague but he took command. He helped Tim, and Mrs. Macpherson half-carried Alan to the courtyard where they were propped against the far wall. The moonlight shone on the Rolls and its two rusty companions and above the stars looked far away and uncaring.

Little flower-like flames were licking out of the hole in the roof and smoke rose white against the night sky.

Tim lay back, feeling dizzy and stroking Lucy, who was whining now and coughing. He touched the kitten, who spat and bit him and this somehow reassured him of life and reality. It seemed impossible that he and the ragged boy had rescued Alan and finding the jewels was now only a dream-like idea from far away.

'Ben, where are you going?' he heard Mum shout.

'Back for them.'

Tim sat up again. There was some kind of struggle going on between Mum and Becca. Suddenly a jet of sparks shot into the sky from the roof, like fireworks. Alan lay wheezing a few feet away.

Becca still struggled. 'Let me go too,' she shouted.

Then the moonlight showed him Mrs. Macpherson's face—not Mum's. Nobody else was there.

'Where's Mum?' he croaked.

'Back in the house,' screamed Becca. 'She and Dad'll be killed.'

Tim began to shake. 'Help them,' he said uselessly and it was then he saw the fire had spread to the orchard . . . flames spurted up above the wall. He heard the soldiers shouting, shouting . . .

Everything went black.

CHAPTER TWELVE

He opened his eyes. Cold, cold . . . he was deadly cold and yet his face burned. He felt for Lucy and the kitten and pulled the reassuring warmth of fur into his arms.

'She's dead,' someone near him was saying.

Dark figures bent over a shape on the ground.

He remembered. 'Mum!' and he struggled dizzily to his feet. Dad was there, holding him.

'She's here! She's all right,' he said.

Torches shone.

What was happening? Sam crouched over Tara, nearby. Mr. Scott, Mum and Becca were looking down at dog and girl and behind them, flames leaped from the roof of the house.

'I've done First Aid,' he heard Sam say. He felt so dizzy . . .

'I can't hold them.' Tim put Lucy and the kitten in Dad's arms.

Then the fire-engine arrived.

He must have half-fainted again because he was next conscious of being carried into an ambulance, past the juddering fire-engine and the firemen. 'It's all right,' Mum was saying as they put him on a kind of bed and she tried to stop him when he struggled to sit up as another stretcher was arriving.

The Rolls swept past at speed. Becca appeared with Dad, crying. 'Tim, where's Tim?' she shouted wildly. 'Is he all right?'

'I'm here,' he said. Could that really be Becca, crying for him? 'Are the animals all right?'

'Fine,' said Dad. 'Sam did something . . . kiss of life, I think, to Tara. Now her father's taking her to the hospital for a small burn. Everything's under control.'

Tim's sliding, confused thoughts settled here a moment. His vague father had changed. Now he was brisk, efficient, in charge. How strange people were, he thought, as the ambulance men brought Alan to join him.

'This is for kids!' Alan's hoarse voice was furious as he looked round the big ward.

Tim opened his swollen eyes. They felt gritty, uncomfortable, and the skin on his face was tight and hot, like sunburn. He dimly remembered last night the doctor in Casualty had said it was heat-flash or something like that and they'd bathed his face with cold water. Alan's face was red and shiny too and the front of his hair was singed.

He looked round the ward. There was a small child rattling the bars of a cot, further down, and a little boy to his right, with his leg in a pulley. Opposite was a strange-looking girl with funny hair and a huge gauze dressing on her nose.

'How do you like my disguise?' Sam croaked. She waved a bandaged hand.

Alan stared. 'How did you get burned?' he asked. 'I thought . . .' then he couldn't stop coughing.

'She went back for Tara,' Tim explained.

'Tara, is she . . .?' Alan couldn't go on.

'She's alive. Dad helped me get her out—she'd been trapped under a heavy old picture.'

Tim thought of that first Alan's portrait.

Sam's hair had been singed off in chunks. 'A bit of hot plaster fell on me,' she said. 'That's why I look funny. Well, Tara didn't seem to be breathing outside so I gave her the kiss of life. We learned it at Red Cross class. If she'd not come round I'd not have let my daddy drive me to the hospital.'

'You were daft. Might have been killed,' Alan grunted.

'It's not only you Scots who love dogs—we Americans do too,' Sam snapped. 'Anyway, I'm a Scott aren't I?' she giggled.

Alan smiled and then Tim saw him turn his face away. He must be crying.

'Everyone's all right,' Tim said, trying to think what to say.

Alan would not look up. 'I started the fire,' he muttered.

Then they were interrupted by a nurse taking their temperatures, followed by washing and breakfast.

Alan still wouldn't speak when Mum, Mrs. Macpherson and Mr. Scott hurried into the ward. Mum explained that Dad and Becca had stayed at Archnacross to keep an eye on the animals and tidy up. Mrs. Macpherson said the fire was well and truly out but all the unused part of the house was in ruins. 'At least it didn't spread—the stone passage-way between the two parts saved the rest of the house,' she said. 'And those campers, Poppy and Tom, were marvellous. They stayed, when we went outside, pouring water down the hall and throwing it against the walls. They've gone now—I wanted them to stay.'

Alan sat up. 'Mr. Scott—you and Sam saved Tara,' he said. 'You were very brave.' Then he lay back, exhausted.

'And he woke us all up, banging on the door,' said Mrs. Macpherson.

'How did you see the fire?' Tim wanted to know.

'Sam saw it,' said Mr. Scott.

She grinned. 'Oh, I shouldn't have smiled,' she said. 'It sort of pulls at my skin. Yeah, well, I couldn't sleep—jet-lag still, I suppose, and I looked out of the window where I could see your house and there were flames and people running . . .'

'Nobody running,' said Mrs. Macpherson. 'That was later, when the firemen came. Shadows, I expect.'

Shadows of the past, Tim thought. There hadn't been any big flames at first, just that little one out of Alan's window.

Alan was staring at Sam out of his puffy eyes.

'You couldna' have seen the flames . . .' he began. Then he stopped. His eyes met Tim's. What had she seen, present or past?

'So I woke my daddy and we rang the fire brigade and came straight over,' Sam went on.

'And Tim saved Alan's life,' Mrs. Macpherson said. 'I'll never forget that. He was so brave.'

'I just can't understand how a boy of Tim's build could pull Alan all that way down to the cellar,' said Mr. Scott. 'He must be real strong for his size.'

'I was sort of helped,' Tim mumbled, knowing Alan was listening. Had that other Alan helped him or had he imagined it?

'Helped?' Mrs. Macpherson's cat's eyes were wide.

'I guess really brave people often get extra strength given them when they need it,' said Mr. Scott.

'Maybe he's all muscle,' Sam giggled.

They would never believe in his ghosts, he knew, so he asked, 'How are the animals?'

'Fine,' Mum said. 'Lucy coughs a bit but the kitten seems quite all right.'

'Did you give it milk?'

'We hadn't time, Tim. When we get back . . . Ben might think of it.'

'Might be too late,' Alan said gloomily. 'And it has to feed from a medicine dropper.'

'So you were hiding a wildcat kit from us, Alan,' his mother said gently.

'A real wildcat kit!' Mr. Scott looked excited.

'Your gillie shot the mother,' Alan snapped.

Mr. Scott looked angry. 'If he's against the wildcats, he'll have to go. I've had an idea but I need to talk to Alan about it when he feels a bit better.'

The doctor came round then and said Tim could go home but Alan and Sam must stay another night. 'For observation.'

'If only the hospital weren't twenty miles away,' said Mrs. Macpherson. 'I must go back and feed the hens and milk Flora.'

'I'm not a baby. I can stay here on my own,' Alan said.

'I'll be around,' said Mr. Scott. 'I've things to attend to downtown and I guess I'll put up in an hotel overnight. Then I can come and visit with you two this evening—if you want me to.' He looked uncertainly at Alan.

After a moment's hesitation, Alan said, 'That'll be fine.'

'I'm starving,' said Sam, just as Becca would have done. 'Daddy can bring us in a feast and then we'll all play cards. Give my love to Becca.'

Mrs. Macpherson walked to the ward door with Mr Scott; they were talking in low voices.

'There's a curse on the place,' Alan muttered. 'We'll not find the treasure now.'

'You never know,' Tim said.

This was something he would do on his own and Alan would be happy at last when the treasure was found.

As they drove back in Mrs. Macpherson's car, Tim tried to play back the scene in the graveyard in his head, when Catherine Macpherson had buried the bundle in the grave. It all seemed curiously remote, as if he had seen it weeks ago instead of yesterday. Had he really seen it at all? He yawned and felt immensely tired. The ward last night had been noisy, with the baby crying, and his legs still felt shaky.

Even though he knew about the damage, it was still a shock to see only the skeleton walls and charred timbers steaming under the hot sun. The remaining side of the house looked strange and lonely.

Dad came to meet them with a bucket in his hand. 'I knew I'd milk a cow on this holiday!' he said happily. 'It took ages and she kicked me once!'

Becca came running across the courtyard, carrying a basket of eggs. 'I've not let them out yet ...' she was panting and then she fell over a piece of charred timber and eggs scattered wildly. Tim laughed. 'Well, you might help me,' she snapped. Had she really sounded worried about him last night?

They all picked up any unbroken eggs. 'I was trying to help,' Becca said, red-faced. 'How's Sam—and Alan?'

'Almost better,' Mum said. 'Back tomorrow.'

Dad put his free hand on Tim's shoulder. 'Well done last night,' he said.

'What happened when you and Mum went back into the house?' Tim asked, remembering suddenly as Tara came bounding out of the house. The hair on her tail was singed, giving it a snakelike appearance.

'Alan and Wayland had got Tara as far as the cellar,' Dad said. 'So we helped them out with her.'

'It was a miracle she wasn't badly burned,' said Mum.

Tim was worried. Why hadn't Lucy followed Tara outside? Were they hiding something?

'Is Lucy really all right?' he asked.

'Come and see,' said Becca. 'It was mean of you to keep the kit secret from me, Tim.'

They all went inside. Lucy was curled round in a box by the stove with the kitten, which was sucking at her teat. Tim lifted it off for a moment and its tiny paws went on kneading the air. A drop of milk clung to its mouth.

'She's come into milk!' said Dad. 'I've read about it happening but it must be unusual.'

Lucy whined anxiously until they put the kitten back. Then she licked Tim's dirty smell off it and sighed contentedly as it went on feeding. Her black, rubbery lips were pulled back in a kind of smile, showing her small white teeth.

'What happens when we go home tomorrow?' Becca asked.

Tim had forgotten about going home. 'Can't we stay?' he asked. 'Lucy will be terribly upset if we leave the kit here.'

'We'll talk about it later,' Mum said.

Mrs. Macpherson was saying she must ring the insurance company. 'The building is under-insured, though. I don't think there will be nearly enough money to rebuild that side of the house.'

Tim knew he had to find the treasure or the Macphersons would sell the house and move to the town.

There was no chance of escaping, even after their makeshift lunch of tinned soup and cheese. Mum said he must rest. He would have argued only his legs felt wobbly and he was very tired. He insisted on taking Lucy and the kit with him in their box.

'It's not fair—I wanted to look after them,' Becca whined.

'Be quiet, Becca,' Dad said, with surprising sharpness.

To Tim's surprise, he went to sleep straight away. He dreamed of a big box marked TREASURE, surrounded by flames. Becca was there, jeering, 'You can't get that, wimp!' He dived through the flames, feeling the heat scorch his skin, and he was reaching for the box when he saw the skull again, grinning at him. He woke with a shout to find Lucy barking a sharp warning from her box.

Mum came in with a tray. 'Supper,' she said. 'You must have been dreaming—what a yell!'

'Supper,' he said vaguely. His body was so heavy that it did not belong to him. He rubbed his gritty eyes. When he began to cough, Mum insisted he stayed in bed.

'I can't go home yet, Mum,' he said. 'I must stay here with Lucy and the kit.' And supposing he'd not found the treasure by the time they had to leave?

'We'll talk tomorrow,' she said. She wouldn't go away but sat by his bed, putting a patch on his old jeans. 'I had to throw away the ones you wore in the fire,' she said. 'And you should see the washing we've got. It's a good thing we've got that tumble-dryer at home.'

He clung to the reality of tumble-dryers and forced himself not to think of the fire, or of the graveyard, as he sank into sleep.

Tomorrow . . .

CHAPTER THIRTEEN

The next morning, he woke up to a funny sound. Then he realised it was the kitten, curled up by Lucy and purring faintly, its blue eyes half-closed. She was gently licking its ear.

He lay there, trying to remember everything. He tried to picture Catherine Macpherson on that terrible day. She must have been running across the heather with Alan and the bundle of silver when the soldiers came and then they both doubled back, Alan hiding in the graveyard and Catherine by the water-butt after she had misled the soldiers. After burying the treasure she and Alan had run down to the burn, where she took the shot intended for him. Alan ran off and tried to defend himself at the cave, where he died. Presumably Ian survived the fire, hidden in the cellar.

There was still a strong smell of burning. He supposed now the house was half-ruined on one side, the surveyor would tell Mr. Scott not to buy it. So the Macphersons would be even worse off than before, unless . . .

He heard a car outside and went to the window. It was the Rolls. He looked at his watch and was horrified to find it was ten o'clock! So much for finding the treasure before Alan came back.

Today his legs were his own and his eyes felt better. He dressed and ran downstairs. Sam and Alan were sitting at the kitchen table, drinking tea. The dressing on Sam's nose made her look clownish and she was laughing. Alan was still pale.

'Wonderful English tea out of a real teapot,' Mr. Scott was saying. 'We just have a tea-bag in a cup. Hi, Tim! You look better and so are these two.'

They told him about Lucy feeding the kit and then of course they had to see for themselves.

'Dad's cleaning out the cowshed,' Mum said. 'And wearing his last pair of clean shorts. Typical!'

Tim wanted to go out but Mum made him eat a bowl of porridge. It hurt a bit to swallow but he felt better for food. Then Alan said he was going out. 'If you really feel all right you can let the hens out,' said his mother. 'We all overslept.'

Mr. Scott looked at Alan. 'You'll tell me soon what you've decided?'

Alan stared at him and for a moment his proud, wild look was so like the other Alan that Tim was suddenly fearful for him. There was something secret in the air, a decision to make and yet Alan believed he was haunted by bad luck.

'I'm not allowed to say what they've been talking about,' Sam's black eyes were gleaming.

'You can tell me,' said Becca.

'No!'

Tim heard the girls quarrelling as he followed Alan outside. Maybe he could get away from Alan somehow.

Tara came too and ran to sniff at a half-eaten rat on the steps of the henhouse. Tim looked away, feeling sick, but

Alan turned it over with his foot and then went to the wire. 'Look,' he said. He had patched the hole over temporarily by propping a heavy bit of wood against it, which had been pushed over. They saw the big paw-marks in the damp earth.

'Probably the wildcat's mate,' he said. 'At least he killed a rat for us and not a hen this time.'

'Do you think he's missing his wife and children?' Tim asked.

Alan laughed. 'You townsfolk!' You think animals are like people. If we rear that kit, he might turn on us one day when he gets cross about something.'

'We ought to give him a name,' Tim said, watching the hens rushing down their ramp, happy to be free.

Alan was busy dragging a heavy wooden box up to the gap in the wire. 'I'll have to mend it properly later today,' he said. He was out of breath and not looking well.

'I'll call him Cluny,' Tim said.

'Cluny.' Alan stared. 'Where did you see that name?'

Tim shook his head as if to clear it. 'I don't know. It's a weird name, isn't it? It sort of came into my head.'

'It's not weird at all,' said Alan. 'You ignorant Sassenach! Cluny Macpherson was a famous leader of our clan. I expect you read it in that book. And by the way, where is that stupid dirk?'

Tim couldn't remember. 'I had it last night,' he said. Had he dropped it when he saw the woman and the boy?

'Trust you to lose it,' Alan sneered. His voice was muffled as he collected eggs from the nesting boxes in the henhouse.

Tim was hurt. He'd show Alan!

He ran off to the graveyard. Where had Catherine Macpherson dug? Dewdrops glistened in the long grasses. It looked so different from the graveyard of the Past.

He walked round, staring at the graves. Then he saw rusty metal and the glint of a jewelled handle where Lucy had once sat. He picked up the dirk and looked again at the name on the mossy, tilting headstone. Using the dirk he scratched carefully at the crumbling letters. Now he could read it properly. CLUNY And that was a wildcat on the headstone!

He remembered the letters on the dirk. Now, in the daylight, he made them out, 'Cluny', again.

This . . . this must be the grave of a pet wildcat! He was sure of it. And this was the place where the treasure was buried—it had been a new grave then and the date was 1746, when the cat died. He pulled at tough grasses and weeds and frantically dug with the dirk, jabbing through the earth.

Suddenly the point hit something hard. Was it a stone . . . or? He jabbed again and then tore at the ground with his hands.

'What are you doing?' Alan asked.

Tim turned round. His fingers were deep in the earth and he could feel something lumpy . . .

'I thought we'd finished with kids' stuff like treasure-hunting,' Alan said, but Tara bounded forward and helped dig with eager paws.

Tim saw a dull gleam in the dark earth. 'Here!' he said.

'That silver bowl might be worth quite a bit,' Mrs. Macpherson said.

They had set the treasure out on the kitchen table. Mr. Scott and Sam were there—they had been at the house with the surveyor and planning man when Tim and Alan ran back.

After the earth and small bits of material had been washed off, the treasure did not look very exciting. There was a bowl, six silver spoons with the clan crest, two silver candlesticks and a silver cat, about eighteen inches high.

Tim picked it up. He was disappointed. Where was the gold, the sparkling rings and the necklaces? He had thought Alan might be exaggerating the treasure but this was just dull.

The cat had red eyes. 'Rubies,' Mum said.

'That would be fit for a musuem,' said Mrs. Macpherson.

Tim felt the cat's body and put his finger in its snarling mouth to clear out the rest of the earth.

A crack opened in its belly. He levered at it with his fingers.

'That's real neat!' said Sam as the cat's side opened out like a little door, showing a belly full of blackened sheep's wool. Tim pulled out the wadding, sodden and rotting. Rings, brooches and a glittering necklace fell out.

'Look! Emeralds!' Mum cried after they had washed the jewels. She put the heavy necklace against her throat. Tim took the jewels from her and piled everything in Alan's lap. 'Yours,' he said.

The excitement made Alan cough so he could not answer.

'Where . . .?' asked Mrs. Macpherson.

'In the grave of Cluny the wildcat,' Alan said. 'Buried by my ancestor, Catherine Macpherson, after the '45.'

'Real live treasure!' Mr. Scott looked like an excited boy himself.

'They'll be valuable?' asked Alan.

'I should think so,' said his mother.

'Now I can keep my home,' Alan said. 'It's an omen.'

Mr. Scott's happiness left his face blank.

'So it's no, then?' he said sadly.

'Not exactly.' Alan polished a brooch on his sleeve until the diamonds and sapphires gleamed against the intricate gold setting. 'We'll rent you the land and the ruined side of the house. But we'll keep our own house and use the money from selling the jewels to start rebuilding the castle. Maybe the National Trust would help—as you suggested. Maybe we should give the castle to them. But I shall keep the silver cat for my descendants.' He had been speaking like a man but now he looked at his mother. 'If that's what you want too, Mum,' he added, sounding more like a boy again.

'Yes.' She smiled.

'Fine by me, Alan,' said Mr. Scott. 'I had wanted to buy, not rent, but I can see you must keep this great ancestral inheritance of yours. I had this idea, when I heard about the wildcat kit—I mentioned it to Alan in the hospital—that I'd start a wildlife sanctuary. Nobody would ever disturb the wildcats again. Maybe I could use the restored wing of your house for a kind of hotel for naturalists?' He sounded quite humble and pleading.

Alan winced a little. Tim thought Mr. Scott would have work to do yet, talking him over to his ideas.

'I don't want to change things,' Mr. Scott went on. 'Just keep them as they are. I think Alan believes me. And he's said he might one day come to America to see another specialist about his leg. He needs to be fit if he's going to look after a nature reserve one day.'

Alan drank some water. He looked directly at Mr. Scott. 'I knew when you and Sam rescued Tara, you weren't just all froth and words like I thought at first,' he said. He went up to Mr. Scott and solemnly shook his hand. 'The Laird of Archnacross welcomes you to his home.'

'Thank you,' Mr. Scott said.

Everyone was quiet.

Something made Tim look out of the window. He thought he saw a tattered boy, far off, and a woman, running down the heather. Just as the dark shapes of the soldiers appeared he shouted, 'No!'

They were all staring at him.

'He must be buried with his family,' he said, just as if someone had told him. 'That will give them peace.'

102

CHAPTER FOURTEEN

'The souls of the righteous are in the hands of God,' began
the Minister, as he laid the remains of Alan Macpherson,
who died in the spring of 1746, in a little plot next to the
big family tomb. Tim was very conscious of the separate
new grave on the other side, where Alan's father was
buried.

Becca was there, Sam and her father too, but Mrs.
Macpherson said she would rather stay at home. Tim
guessed she did not want to see her husband's grave again
quite so soon.

Tim's parents had gone back to London but they had
agreed the children could stay with Lucy, until the
kitten was weaned. Tim tried not to think of going back
but at least they were returning for a few days in the
Christmas and Easter holidays, with promise of a longer
time in the summer—when Dad was going to help with
the Wildlife Sanctuary. 'You'll not stand the cold in
winter,' Alan said, typically, but he added, 'Well, bring

that guinea-pig dog. At least she's got long fur,' and he had actually smiled.

'. . . and in the time of their visitation, they shall shine and run to and fro like sparks among the stubble,' the Minister went on now. Tim thought the words must mean the ghosts, flitting over the stubble . . . only here they moved over the heather.

It was a grey morning but now the sun burst through the clouds and he could see it gleaming gold on the Black Loch.

'With His right hand shall He cover them and with His arm He shall protect them.' The Minister had finished.

Alan was crying. Tim knew he cried for his father, not for that long-ago Alan. Mr. Scott moved closer and handed him a large white handkerchief. Alan did not move away. Tim thought he heard the howling of a wildcat. Was it from the Past or the present?

Maybe the past flowed into the present, like the burn forced through its rocky channel to mix with the calm waters of the Black Loch.

There was a feeling of peace in the graveyard and over the heather beyond. Tim looked at the quiet grave; he knew he would not see the ghosts again.

If you liked this book then why not
look out for other Kelpies. There are
more than fifty titles to choose from
and they are available from all good bookshops.

For a free Kelpie badge, catalogue and
any other information, please send
a stamped addressed envelope to:
Margaret Ritchie (K.C.B.)
Canongate Publishing Ltd.,
16 Frederick Street, Edinburgh EH2 2HB